THE OUTLANDER'S GRIT

THE OUTLANDER'S GRIT

MARITES ONG

Andean Publishing
New York

Andean Publishing
1420 York Avenue
New York, NY 10021

Published by Andean Publishing

Book design © 2024 Andean Publishing
www.andeanpublishing.com
THE OUTLANDER'S GRIT / Marites Ong
1 2 3 4 5 6 7 8 9 10

Identifiers:
Library of Congress Control Number: 2024907648
ISBN: 979-8-9905189-3-3 (paperback)
ISBN: 979-8-9905189-4-0 (hardcover)
Printed in the United States of America

Dedication

Jeremy Taylor, thank you for your talents. I am so happy you're my friend. Thank you for your creative design, the execution of the book cover is impeccable.

To those who bullied me and those who are bullying me—beware. You will be the next monster in my story. I will not tell you to stop but beware, my publisher is Russian.

To those who supported me—there's so many of you. I can't mention all of you in this book. Otherwise I don't have anybody to thank for in my next book. But I thank all of you. If you want to be mentioned in my next book—leave a message on my YouTube channel @mo-ex1414. Please like, share, and subscribe. Leave me a thumbs-up, a heart and smile emoji.

CHAPTER ONE

Reception

Olivia wanted to make sure that everything is perfect. She wanted for every guest to be attended for and nobody is neglected. She was busy assisting the hustling and bustling staff with high energy in the bar area, in the kitchen, in the hallway. She realized that she was working like a donkey for that wedding and won't get paid—not even a penny. But and this is with a big but—she will only help pay the bills later.

Then she took a stride to check the parking lot for nothing—but ended up taking a deep breath. With all the medications that she's been taking—making her medicine cabinet look like a pharmacy. Them medications that make her feel groggy at times—she had to get up at 3:30AM to get started with this shindig. She did not set an appointment with the hair stylist and make-up artist because she's comfortable wearing her red matte lipstick and nothing else.

While she was standing at the parking lot, she took notice of the wooden electric lamp post standing directly to the welcome-door of the venue. The tangled electrical wires connected to the lamp post hosted two pigeons perching comfortably. Olivia thought for a moment that it was nice for those two pigeons to join the celebration. She could only pray for the two of them not to get fried. She must have been hallucinating because in her mind the two pigeons looked like they're talking to each other while moving their heads.

In her mind the gray pigeon said, "Look at this wedding, it's another love story that we can only wait if it will last or fail—another fairy tale maybe. Are they going to prioritize their careers and not build a family soon? How long is this show going to play? One will leave the toothpaste open on top of the bathroom counter then they will fight. Then one will forget their anniversary—then comes a huge fight. I wonder if this one had drafted their prenup? I wonder how much money will the divorce lawyers make out of this one?"

White pigeon said, "I know, right. Can you believe that? The wedding that was held here last week—they thought I'm a dove. I know I'm white, but I'm a pigeon not a dove. They kept me in a white cage with another bird—an actual dove. They didn't notice the difference—they didn't care. As long as my color is white that's fine. They made sure though, that we won't escape so they tied a white shimmering ribbon around the cage and fed us with fifteen pieces of beans making sure that none of us won't shit when the bride or the groom set us free during their ceremony. Thank goodness for the fifteen beans, though, otherwise I wouldn't have flown—I would be dazed from hunger. I would have just flapped my wings two times—but I'd make sure I landed on the wedding cake and pecked on the crushed almonds covering it. What a bummer?"

Olivia then came back to her senses, she thought every penny was worth spent for her niece, and bid goodbye to the pigeons. She went back directly to the kitchen directing every staff where each piece of whatever item was to be placed on its rightful spot. Everybody wanted everybody to have fun and celebrate the day.

It was a day when the sun decided to showcase its full strength—rays of blinding light yet a moderate welcoming warmth. Mother nature was now motivated to exhibit its splendid beauty and vibrant colors, pleasing the eyes of those who purposefully loved the organic form of the earth. After the cold days that tormented the aching bones and muscles of senior citizens Julieta and Olivia, the days finally began to warm up. Moreover, it was not only a beautiful day—it was when Dana finally tied the knot with Alwyn.

They have all the reasons to rejoice—the whole family was there. Their friends were present to witness two lives were joining together as one. The wedding's theme of color was light cerulean blue. An enchanting color seemingly blanketing the earth as if the sky couldn't stop its generosity in sharing its magnificent hue, up where it belongs and down where it's borrowed.

There were twelve round tables which were covered with crisp white table cloths seating ten people each. The flower ball centerpieces were a mix of silk flowers and natural greeneries. Every table setting was perfectly put together for a feasting style. The ice sculpture was on display at the center of the dessert station with sweet treats in white and sky-blue colors were arranged at its foot for the guests to enjoy.

Dana was beaming in her pure white princess tulle bridal gown. It was high-neck, see-through long sleeved, embellished with blending of beads and appliqué. It has covered button closures, and she wore a gorgeous cathedral veil.

As the mother of the bride, Julieta was wearing a spaghetti strapped A-line satin dress. She purposely covered her arms and shoulders with a long-sleeved lace bolero. But Julieta was torn between the excitement of Dana's wedding and the anguish of her beloved's heart.

CHAPTER TWO

Budding Hope

Roberto dreamt of having a good life. What is a good life anyway? Nobody could have escaped the imperfections of the world we're living in. He needed a job that would enable him to live comfortably. A means where he could plan his finances—paying his bills, save a little, ensure himself that he's got money to pay his mortgage if ever he got into it and go on vacation even if it's just a week's vacation every year. That could have been a good life for him. Was it too much to ask?

He needed to help his family in his country, too. He had four sisters and a brother. His second born sister, Claudia, died due to complications of diabetes when she was 42. Roberto witnessed her suffering in his younger years, he helped his Mom when

Claudia was in the hospital for two months. His Mom spent Christmas and New Year's day in the hospital with her. Roberto's Mom and other sisters took turns in helping out. Claudia can't eat just any food like she used to. She has to be eating specific diet not to increase her creatinine level. She went through dialysis while she was in the hospital. The doctors wanted to ensure that they give Claudia the best care they could—to make her well again, to keep her alive, to make her live her best life again.

CHAPTER THREE

Pinching Pain

It was one early morning—Claudia asked Roberto for a sip of water.

Claudia said: "I'm thirsty, is there any water left in the cup?"

Roberto answered: "Yes there is."

Roberto placed the plastic straw into Claudia's mouth. She began to sip, she finished about an ounce of water and Roberto took the plastic straw off her mouth and placed the cup on top of the arm chair of his seat. All of a sudden Claudia started to convulse. He didn't know what to do, he thought it was just normal. He didn't call the nurses right away. But his heart was beating fast and his mind was in doubt— he finally had the guts to call the nurses' attention who was assisting another patient close by. Due to financial difficulties, Claudia was confined in a charity ward. It was a big room that accommodated ten patients with different health conditions.

Claudia was breathing but her inhaling and exhaling were too slow. The nurses panicked. Taking her pulse made them all rushed in to get the portable AED. They tried three times to shock her. No matter what the medical staffs did, Claudia lost her battle. The doctor pronounced her expired after an hour.

Roberto has been in the United States for 20 years. Within two decades, he worked at different restaurants, bodegas and landscaping companies and tried doing business on his own but failed. He couldn't hold on to any drop of confidence because he's missing an immigration status. What he believed was this status was the only thing that will bring him good luck. He thought, if there was no bad luck—he wouldn't have any luck at all.

CHAPTER FOUR

Grindstone Streak

Roberto worked as the grill man at McDonald's along Garden State Parkway in Union. His boss—Troy, was kind to him somehow. He was a tall, dark and burly guy with bald head. He talked with a bit-of a baritone voice. He loosely wears his uniform shirt tucked in his baggy pants. It was required to wear a slip-resistant shoes but Troy wore a pair of black Niké sneakers which was non-compliant to one of the rules. Troy was mostly on top of every-thing at work. He knew when to holler at the ca-shier and the line staff when the drive-through was backed up. He'd shout if the burgers on the warmer were too much or too little in count. But it was clear that he lives under the skirt of his wife—Floreana.

The wife of Roberto's boss doesn't like him. Floreana wasn't pretty but not ugly, regular maybe, but tremendously insecure. She wears her dark brown hair in a hairnet under her McDonald's uniform hat. Her pale complexion and big eye-bags made Roberto believe that she cannot get a goodnight sleep every time. No matter how much she tried to hide those eye-bags under two layers of concealer and five layers of foundation—Roberto knew that she's not getting laid at night—she's not getting laid at all.

The wife was giving Roberto a hard time—not a hard on—but a hard time at work. She would always line up four to five tasks even before he clocked in for work. Floreana would have to make Roberto go out in the dining area to sweep and mop the floor plus empty the garbage bins out, replace the garbage bins with fresh bags then take them all out in the dumpster. All these tasks were waiting for Roberto—nobody else was sent out to check the cleanliness of the dining not until Roberto's shift starts.

After finishing up the dining, he needed to clean the bathrooms, put away all cleaning tools and supplies. She would have him go in the freezer and organize the boxes and refill all stations with necessary supplies. All these needed to be done in an hour.

Roberto was a grill man not a custodial—that's how much of a slave driver Floreana was.

She only did that tactic with Roberto to torment him. She knew he was smarter than the other employees. She feared that if Roberto gained more knowledge and tenure, she could be kicked out of her job for a lesser hourly rate. Roberto only received minimum wage, but for a cheaper pay rate he's a fast learner. Roberto thought it was discrimination—but he didn't take it too seriously. He knew that if he can't take it anymore, he can always quit.

It was one morning when he felt that he can't take her demands anymore, it was just too much to put up with. He was scared that he might just end up picking a fight with a lady boss, he thought it was better to leave. He quit.

He applied for a job at the pizza store, where he saw a 'Now Hiring' sign.

He went to the store to submit his resume, he asked the woman at the counter, "Hi, what is the position that you guys needed for the 'Now Hiring' sign by the door?"

The counter woman said, "Hi, I'm Marlenny, we need a dishwasher. It's kinda hard for them guys to come by, you know. Everybody wants to be a counter-person, I keep on telling them that I am 'it'. They ain't getting my job."

Roberto chuckled, "Oh that's great, I believe I can do that job. Here's my resume, my contact number is in there. I hope you would call me, in case I need to be interviewed."

Marlenny said, "Wait a minute, wait. I'll call the boss, if he's not busy he will talk to you. If he is, then I would have to call you later."

Roberto said, "Ok, I can wait. I have time."

Marlenny hollered, "Boss. I need you here."

Boss Gerry walked to the counter and asked, "What is it?"

Marlenny handed him the resume and said, "This boy's applying for the dishwasher position that we needed to fill since twenty-five years ago."

Boss Gerry asked Roberto, "Do you have experience in the kitchen, how about dishwashing job experience?"

Roberto answered, "I worked at McDonalds as a grill man, I know I can be a dishwasher. That's part of my tasks there anyway, although it's not my main job but it's part of the job."

Boss Gerry said, "When can you start?"

Roberto asked, "How about today?"

Boss Gerry said, "Marlenny will show you the ropes."

Marlenny hollered one more time, "Hey Renz it's garbage day tomorrow. Don't forget to take the bins out at 4PM today. And don't you wait for me to take them out otherwise my uterus will come out of my asshole—them heavy shit."

Renz replied with a chuckle, "I've been taking them out, you're the one volunteering putting them out by the curb."

Marlenny couldn't help herself, "Oh yeah smarty pants. If I didn't put them out by the curb last week no one would. Everybody's always waiting for me to do shit around here, I don't understand why everybody forgets everything. Renz sweetheart, I'm old enough to be your gramma. Tell the rest of the kitchen not to forget what I just said, ok? That uterus ain't comin' out from Mars—it ain't coming out of Uranus either. It's comin' out of mine. Get it done, will yah!"

Renz could only reply with a big smile on his face, "Yeah, junior boss. Oh, before I forget, hey Boss Gerry, we need a new broom. The one we have in the kitchen is on life support for a while now. It's making me recall the memories when I lost my two front teeth—I was seven years old that time. When

I bite a donut there's space on my bite mark. That broom lost its soul forty-eight years ago, Boss. Oh, and junior boss—I'll tell the kitchen. Hey kitchen, hhheeeyyy kitchen..."

Boss Gerry couldn't control his laughter, happy tears were coming out of the corner of his eyes. He walked away and headed back to the office giggling—his shoulders jerking up and down.

Roberto got the job. All the years living without a legal status was super scary for him. Every day of his life he was afraid. He always had to look over his shoulder if something was going on, somebody was following him, if immigration was at his ass. He can't eat without immigration on his mind, can't sleep without thinking about immigration, every morning he awoke from slumber—still immigration.

SIDE COMMENT: He better get-hitched
with immigration if he can't live without it.
Damn immigration you better loosen up.

CHAPTER FIVE

Health Conditions

He lived in Union for five years, when his Dad, who was in his home country started to get very ill. His Dad—Leandro was diagnosed with pharyngeal cancer. As Leandro got older, he developed heart disease without the family catching it at an early stage. Leandro had the procedure of getting the cancer arrested. But his heart fainted, he had a stroke, one too many times before. But the last one was a real strike—Roberto's Dad got bedridden. He can't feed himself anymore, can't stand, can't shower by himself anymore, can't do anything for himself, 100% incapacitated. His Mom and oldest sister, Maybel were the ones left to take care of his Dad. His other siblings were around, but could only do so much. The whole family gathered around to take turns in helping. Roberto could only worry so much for he's too far away from his family.

He was sending money to support his Mom—more now than before. He started sending Vitamin supplements for both his parents. His support had gotten generous, when the time that his Dad got very sick—and there was no way of reversing everything that happened to his Dad. He worried for his Mom—she might not bear the burden she would collapse.

His sister, Rizza was suffering from the clutch of diabetes. Rizza was the third born child of his parents. Although Roberto was worried about his Dad, he was worried about his sister too. He wanted to think about them, but he needed to think about himself too.

CHAPTER SIX

Dwelling Overcast

He lived on the second floor of a one family house. The second floor was the attic converted into two-bedroom flat accommodating two tenants. He kept his job at the pizza store as a dishwasher. Even though he earned a Bachelor's Degree in Computer Engineering from his country. He did not think about his diploma. All for him was to earn a living—not prostituting his own fleshly being. He didn't care what kind of work he does, as long as it's an honest way of earning money.

He worked hard, always on time and not complaining. The pizza store was just close by his house, in the same street but one mile away. He doesn't really have a problem with commute because buses 66 and 94 passed by pretty regularly in front of the store. At times he opted to take the bus because of knee pain, foot pain, leg pain and what have you.

His landlord and landlady were kind to him at first. They supported his being out of status. They said it wasn't a problem, all they care about was for him to pay his rent—cash and on time. He did not see life like it was hard. He kept working, did not think of taking vacations nor requesting for extra days off. As a matter of fact, he kept taking on schedules that were left by his coworkers when they don't show up. He respected his boss, he respected his job.

He started to earn a little bit more than what he used to get when Boss Gerry gave him a raise. It was only half a buck but it helped him in more ways than anybody else would consider. He got paid cash as a dishwasher and he was able to really budget his money. With the raise that he got from the company—he was able to put aside fifty cents per hour and put them in a plastic quart take-out container. He sure could use the money for his family, but it's also fair that he had something for himself. He was able to save a minimum of twenty dollars a week. He thought he'd use that money for himself. He'd order new shirts from Macy's Online for himself that he can afford not exceeding twenty dollars each time.

His delivery got pretty regular, it caught the eyes, of the woman who was living down stairs. She was the Mom of two girls, her husband doesn't have a job but busy taking care of the kids more than anything else.

Since the landlord and the landlady were living in their own house three blocks away from where Roberto lived, the woman who lived down stairs snitched to the landlady. Gemma was a short, stocky, black haired, nurse. She's got confidence that made her feel gorgeous—so gorgeous that anyone can hear the whiplash when she turns around. She worked as a private nurse to a patient in Clinton, NJ. She was chasing time—finishing her shift when she stepped wrong and fell from the stairs. She took an early retirement due to the ankle injury she encountered at the patient's house.

Gemma called Landlady Josephine and said, "Roberto has been receiving a couple of deliveries from Macy's Online lately. He's got money, otherwise he won't buy anything if he's broke."

Landlady Josephine said, "Oh really? Let me see if he can afford to pay an extra twenty-five dollars more for his rent. Maybe I'll wait two months more before I break it to him. Thanks for the input."

Gemma said, "Sure thing."

He kept working—it didn't matter if he was in a closing schedule or opening. All he thought was save—and the perk of saving his fifty cents an hour.

His landlady, more like Cruella de Vil, sent him a text message.

Landlady Josephine asked, "Hey Roberto, are you at home?"

Roberto replied, "I am at work right now. I will be done in two hours. Is there a problem in the rooming house?"

Landlady Josephine texted, "No, I just want to know if I can visit you today. My husband and I have some pastries for all of our tenants and I thought to bringing it for you.

Roberto replied, "Oh thank you, maybe you can put it in the fridge and I'll check it out as soon as I get home."

Landlady Josephine said, "We will be there—if you're not home yet, we'll wait for you."

Roberto replied, "Ok, I'll see you then."

When Roberto reached the house, he took his key from his backpack and opened the front door. He climbed the fifteen-step stairs and unlock the upstairs door. He saw his landlady sitting on the chair facing the dining table, facing the wall. She had a pen on her right hand and a piece of printing paper on the table where she was writing stuff that he couldn't read. His landlord was fixing the faucet by the sink in the bathroom. The toolbox was on the floor in front of the bathroom door.

He asked his landlady, "What's going on here? Is there a problem in the bathroom faucet? It was working fine this morning when I used it. I am sure there's no problem with it when I left."

Landlady Josephine said, "We are putting new hard wares before any of them gets worn out. We'd like to maintain the house in good condition any way so we're doing this."

Roberto asked, "Is it going to be finished today?"

Landlady Josephine said, "Yes, my husband is almost done with the work. I didn't hire a plumber because it's expensive. The reason why I wanted to see you is because I am going to raise your rent for another twenty-five dollars a month for maintenance like this. Good thing that my husband knows how to fix simple things like this, otherwise it would have been more money to pay the plumber."

Roberto said, "Will it be alright if I just paid for the new hardware that you put in? It doesn't cost that much if you're asking me for another twenty-five dollars a month, right?"

Landlady Josephine said, "This is not the only repairs we will be putting in. We still have to repaint the sidings and the sidewalk needs new slabs."

Roberto said, "Isn't that your responsibilities, not mine?"

Landlady Josephine said, "We don't live here, you guys do—those are all on you not us. After all, we don't want the authorities coming over here and do some inspections, right?"

Roberto said, "Ok yes, of course."

Landlady Josephine then said, "Your pastry is in the fridge just like you requested."

Roberto walked to the fridge and opened the door, he saw the pastry and said, "Thank you, I'll eat it later."

Landlady Josephine said, "We're done here now, the next month that your due—it will be twenty-five dollars more, okay?"

Roberto did not respond. As soon as the owners left the place, he opened bedroom number one, where he lived and placed his backpack at the foot of his bed. He went out to sit on the chair where his landlady sat and thought his responsibility became a bit heavier. He kept thinking about how to budget again. He thought he needed to stop the Macy's Online order to cover for the raise of the rent. He thought again that he can cover for the raise even if he would still order some stuff for himself. As soon as the light bulb in his head lit, bedroom number two opened its door and out another tenant. Ronald was taller at 6'2" while Roberto was 5"11'. They both have brown skin tone, Ronald was buffed Roberto was slim.

Ronald asked, "Hey man, what's up?"

Roberto said, "I think the rent was up."

Ronald said, "What do you mean the rent was up?"

Roberto said, "The owners were just here, fixing the bathroom faucet."

Ronald said, "They did? I didn't hear a beat. I was so tired man, I don't know if I can still do the graveyard shift. I might request for a morning shift or a mid-shift or something. I'm off today, I slept all day, I was so tired—I can't even take a leak."

Roberto said, "It's part of maintenance that's why the rent went up for another twenty-five dollars."

Ronald was awakened when he heard it, "Oh flipping snap. This is all your freaking fault."

Roberto said, "What? What have I done? How did it become my fault?"

Ronald said, "You have been receiving Macy's Online orders delivered here. They have never seen you order anything once or twice a month—regularly and I mean regularly. They know you have money—they know you can afford it. Instead of you buying shit online—they'd rather collect that money from your pocket than for you to give it to any store. Flipping shit. That's how they are, and the people downstairs are the informants especially the woman. You've been here five years, you don't know? I have been here three years I noticed right away. They are gangsters, oh men. All they want is money, if they see you have it—they'll take it from yah. How do you think they pay for their BMW and Mercedes Benz? You know their kids have good jobs, but they won't spend their money. They will take it from us to sustain their lifestyles. Flipping greedy asses."

Roberto said, "Oh man, sorry. I haven't been paying attention to anything. I thought I'd just go to work pay my rent, keep the house clean, keep the bathroom clean, keep my room clean and that's it. I didn't really know they are keeping an eye on us. That's freaky, that's selfish."

Ronald said, "Now what do we do? I got a plan, we can break the faucet every month so we have new faucet every month. It's part of the maintenance, right? We'll tell them that they are buying cheap faucets that's why it keeps on breaking. This is just between you and me, if they learned about this—we only have ourselves to blame."

Roberto laughed, he thought it was a bright idea but won't participate. He thought if the faucet got broken then it's broken. He was scared of the authority's part of his conversation with Landlady Josephine. He's thinking about, how come Ronald was not afraid of the owners, and how come he's so scared. He can't parallel their lives. He thought he needed to be more like Ronald, he's got to stop being afraid—he's been living that kind of life for a long time. What needed change? He lost his appetite, he lost his energy, he took the pastry from the fridge. He opened it then sunk his teeth to devour the little piece of plain sweet bread called pastry.

CHAPTER SEVEN

Crowded Thoughts

He went to work the following day. He dropped the pizza pans on the floor—it created a big sound—like a Gong was hit to start the Sumo wrestling competition. A bucket slipped from his hands and the silverwares dove on the floor. He tried to focus, but it was obvious—he wasn't himself. His coworkers took notice, so did Boss Gerry. The big man approached Roberto.

Boss Gerry asked, "Roberto, my man. How are you? You sick or hungry? Something is going on. What's up?"

Roberto turned the faucet off—he said, "Boss sorry, I was just thinking about something."

Boss Gerry said, "I know you're thinking about something, otherwise I wouldn't have heard a sounding Gong. And then the knives and forks swam in the waterless floor. Some problem? Women?"

Roberto said, "Nothing boss, it's nothing."

Boss Gerry said, "How about if I fire you, right here, right now?"

Roberto said, "I just received notice from the owners that the rent would hike up again."

Boss Gerry, "I knew that word 'fire' will open your mouth. You told me before that your rent will raise—when was that, two years ago?"

Roberto said, "Yeah, something like that. Two and a half years ago."

Boss Gerry said, "Then they will raise it again? Your owners are nothing but scum of the earth. They are not greedy but super greedy. You've been there, what, five years? You've been paying your rent like a heart-beat—you've never skipped one. And this is what they'll do to you? They treat you like they're operating a legal rental house—that's an illegal rooming house you're living in. Why are they doing this to you? I'd tell yah, those people are scumbags."

Roberto sigh, "I can't do anything boss, they said they wanted the authorities to see the place neat and clean."

Boss Gerry said, "Flipping harassment, they're trying to scare you. That's their tactic. How I wished your situation would flip. You're the owner and they're the tenant—I wonder how they'd feel about it. Don't worry, if anybody calls out—I'll call you. Just don't get sick ok?"

Roberto said, "Ok boss, I won't. Thank you."

Boss Gerry said, "You're my one big Achilles heel. You know it and I know, you know that I know it. But you never take advantage of anyone of us here in the store. That's why I like you. I'm Italian—your enemy is my enemy. But don't get any more of them, friends are better to collect."

Roberto answered with a chuckle and said, "Yes boss."

They laughed—Boss Gerry said, "If you want to take a slice of pizza—go to the front counter and ask Marlenny. If you're worried that you might not finish your work on time, stay until you finish your job and take home some pizza or a calzone which ever you want. That's all I can compensate you for, I'd like to keep on giving you raise but you understand I can't, right? So instead of buying anything that you want to eat for dinner or whatever, take home some stuff, not all of them but some stuff. Ok?"

Roberto couldn't be happier, but his responsibilities are real for him. He needed to stop thinking about his Mom and Dad but he can't. He needed to think of himself first but he kept putting himself last. He was finishing his work and his mind was budgeting his salary for rent, for his family, and for his bills. How will he be able to do that? That was a question he needed to answer.

SIDE COMMENT: Maybe he can borrow the Cloak of Invisibility from Harry Potter to rob a bank. No, he can't do that. What if he disguised himself as homeless and started pan handling, he can't do any of that Roberto was too timid, he's not a good actor—he's very transparent.

He worked six days a week, but not 72 hours work-shift. Boss Gerry needed to give him a breather. He's a good worker but he can't get exhausted from it—otherwise he might break, Boss Gerry knew it.

CHAPTER EIGHT

Remembering Helping

He had a day off, this was the only day that he can really run his errands. The laundromat was a little over half mile from where he lived. It was easy to walk over there if he doesn't have any carry-on. But if there was a load of laundry on his shoulder, one can only bet it's a feat.

He went early to the laundromat with his dirty clothes in a black zippered laundry duffle. He loaded the washer, he poured his detergent and fabric softener in their respective compartments. He dropped the coins in and the machine started. He waited for the Variety Store to open, it was just across from the laundromat. As soon as the store opened—he crossed the street, went in the store and approached the cashier.

Roberto said: "Good morning, I need to send money by Western Union, is it up or down?"

Cashier said: "It's up today, thank goodness. It's been down yesterday and the day before."

The cashier handed out a Western Union form for him to fill out. As soon as he's done writing all the information—he handed the form back to the cashier. She entered all the information into the system, collected the money from Roberto and handed him the receipt. He needed to send money so his Mom can buy what his Dad needed. He finished his laundry chore and went home. He hanged his shirts, folded his pants and he put away his underclothes in a dark blue plastic organizer with lid. He decided to go out of the house again.

Gemma noticed that he hasn't been receiving any deliveries lately. But she noticed that he's been going out more. She knew when Roberto's working and when he's not working. He's not wearing his uniform that time—it meant he's not heading for work.

SIDE COMMENT: When will these people be nice to others, when will these people mind their own business? They need to keep their noses off Roberto's ass.

CHAPTER NINE

Fattening Purse

Roberto walked to Morris Avenue with his back-pack slung to both shoulders, he waited for the 114 bus, New York bound and boarded. He went to Union Center to visit the dollar store to buy some toiletries. He knew he had some time, so he walked around as if he was sight-seeing. He saw a hair salon, he went inside and saw that there were people in line waiting for their turn, men and women alike. He walked out and tried the other one across the street near the movie house. He went in and the hairstylist was almost done with her client. She looked at Roberto and wondered what did he want. She run the hair dryer on the client's shoulder to clean up, she collected the payment and the client left.

Roberto knew she's older but doesn't look like one from where he was standing—almost four feet away. She approached him, then he saw the wrinkle on her face disguised under the two layers of foundation.

Hairstylist Mhargie asked, "Do you have an appointment?"

Roberto said, "No, I was just walking around and decided to get a haircut."

Hairstylist Mhargie said, "I really don't take walk-ins but my other client cancelled her appointment so I'll take you in. For now, you can get a haircut, next time you need to set an appointment, ok?"

Roberto said, "Ok, I didn't know. I always buzz my hair myself. I have a razor at home, but today I can't do it. I want to be out of the house. I can't stay in it all the time. I thought I need to go somewhere else today to chill."

Hairstylist Mhargie said, "Oh ok, I hope I'd see you more often, though. You can style your hair more than just a buzz cut, you know."

Hairstylist Mhargie told Roberto to sit on the revolving chair. He complied. A blue cape flung on his face and was fastened around his neck. Hairstylist Mhargie was prepping her tools when a couple of women entered the salon. They were chattering their way in, one wore the silvery color of her hair very beautifully, she's slim, not tall, but pretty. Even with the wrinkle on her face and the evident crows' feet on the corners of her eyes. The other one looked like an inch taller, brunette, looked like younger than the other.

Hairstylist Mhargie took the water spray bottle and started wetting Roberto's head.

Hairstylist Mhargie said, "Oh the sisters, welcome."

Roberto asked, "Oh no, they were your clients on the schedule?"

Hairstylist Mhargie said, "No, I love gossiping with them, that's why they're here. The older one with the silver hair is Olivia and the other one is Julieta."

Julieta asked, "Sister Mhargie what happened with my request?"

Hairstylist Mhargie asked, "What request?"

Julieta said, "The house cleaner that I requested you to make an inquiry on. I need help cleaning the house, you know for a fact that I am not good at it. The house is a mess right now, I need somebody to clean it. Even Dana who barely goes home, is asking me about it."

Hairstylist Mhargie said, "Rose wasn't available, she has an assignment as of now. I can't possibly pull her out to clean your house. Give me a little bit more time.

Olivia butted, "I need help too, I'm too old to clean the house. Before my knee replacement I can do anything at my age. But now—forget it."

Julieta said, "You know for a fact that we're both seniors now. Although Olivia stopped working—I won't let myself stop. What am I going to do in the house? Clean the house all day? That's why I kept my part time job."

Roberto's mind was playing tricks on him, he debated if he would take the cleaning-job. He was thinking, were they going to trust him if he cleaned their houses because he's a man. Thoughts were playing in his mind, his Dad, his Mom, his whole family. But he can't have days off from the pizza store any more, maybe he can—all he had to do was talk to Boss Gerry. His mind was flooding with all these thoughts.

Until he blurted out, "I think I can do that job."

The three women were all quiet, thinking about how to process the sound that they just heard. They looked at each other with faces that resembled an expression like their mouths were filled with Sour Patch gummy worms.

Hairstylist Mhargie said, "Wait, wait. We don't know you. We need to know the person whom we're going to let in our houses."

Roberto said, "I thought it's the two of them who needed help, you too?"

Hairstylist Mhargie said, "The deal is—if I found someone, that person will clean my apartment too."

Roberto said, "I think I can manage three houses. I work for the pizza store by Vauxhall Road."

Julieta said, "Your boss is Gerry?"

Roberto exclaimed with happiness, "Yes, he's my boss, he's an awesome guy."

Julieta said, "When can you start?"

Olivia said, "Wait, hold your horses, we don't know him."

Julieta asked, "How long have you been working with Gerry?

Roberto answered, "Almost two years and counting."

Julieta said, "Yeah we don't know this dude, but we know Gerry. He's been working with Gerry that long, it means Gerry trusts him. I trust whoever Gerry trusts. Can you clean my house tomorrow?"

Roberto said, "After my haircut I can go to your house and clean until maybe 10PM today—I am available."

Julieta said, "Sister why don't you hurry up and finish that hair—and I will take this awesome bozo to my house. I won't leave until your head gets done, boy. I am taking you to my house, I really need help."

Olivia said, "You can't—not today. We need to go to Woodbridge remember?"

Julieta said, "Oh shit, I forgot. I was excited for this boy to clean the house. Ok, not today. Next week if you can make it. By the way what's your name?"

Roberto replied, "My name is Roberto, can I get paid cash for that cleaning? Boss Gerry pays me cash since the time I started working for him."

Julieta said, "How come I've never seen you there before?"

Roberto said, "I work in the kitchen, I'm always in the kitchen. We're always busy there, I work as the dishwasher. I can only do the cleaning on my day off. I can do two houses on my one day off. I can squeeze the other one, when I get a morning off before I go to Boss Gerry's. Or I can squeeze one when I get an afternoon off from the pizza store. I think I need to see the extent of cleaning I need to do, and how big are your houses."

Julieta said, "My house is small, I only have the main floor for you to clean. I have two bedrooms, one bathroom, the living room, dining room and the kitchen. It's fairly small, manageable—I guess you can get done in six hours, tops."

Olivia said, "Mine is bigger than her house, you might need eight hours to clean it."

Roberto said, "So you want me to clean your house too? I know you can trust me, but do you?"

Olivia said, "I'll take what Julieta said. Gerry trusts you—I think I can trust you."

Roberto said, "Good, can I take my head back now?"

Hairstylist Mhargie said, "My apartment is small, but I have two floors. Three bedrooms upstairs, downstairs there's a small office, then the living room and the dining room. You don't have to clean the two bedrooms. My tenants were responsible for theirs. You only have to clean my bedroom and the bathroom upstairs and the rest of the cleaning will take place on the first floor."

Roberto asked, "Who's Julieta, and who's Olivia?"

Julieta introduced herself, Olivia followed and then Hairstylist Mhargie. Roberto was beaming inside. His heart leaped for joy, he doesn't want them to see the happiness he felt, but he's also thinking that it might be overwhelming for him. He thought—he will cross the bridge when he got there. In the meantime, he found himself a part time job. He loved the decision he made to get a haircut.

CHAPTER TEN

Fixing Schedules

The following day he asked permission from Boss Gerry.

Roberto asked, "Hey boss, how are you? I bet we'll be busy today. There's a game at the high school later. People might want to order pizza."

Boss Gerry said, "Oh yeah that's right, shit I forgot about that. I'll ask Renz to pick up two extra sacks of flour from the house and I'll prep the dough, we'll see how it goes. How are you?"

Roberto said, "I'm ok boss, I'd like to request for a Wednesday AM shift permanently, and a Thursday days-off permanently if that's ok with you?"

Boss Gerry said, "Yeah that's fine we'll manage. Why? What are you up to? You found another job? You're leaving me?"

Roberto said, "No boss. I just have some stuff, I thought Thursdays is perfect. It's not one of our busy days anyway. If I get my rest Thursdays then I'm ok Fridays which is a busy day."

Boss Gerry said, "Fair enough. Do you want to start next week?"

Roberto said, "Yes boss, that would be great."

Boss Gerry said, "Ok then, you're off Thursdays."

He finished his shift. He went home with a whistle on his back. He's got to figure out how to tell the ladies that he can do it. He didn't get their phone numbers. He thought of walking back to the hair salon and get the number that was advertised on the glass window. He can't wait to go back there, he was excited.

Early in the morning before he started his gig at the pizza store again, he took the bus. Good thing he caught it—otherwise it's a 45-minute walk going one way and another 45 to go back. He saved the phone number in his cell phone.

It was 8AM he was debating if he would send a text message at that hour. He sent one anyway, his phone beeped, he read the message. The phone number he's sending a text message to was a landline.

He talked to himself, "Oh darn. Oh ok—good thing it's a landline. I won't have to worry if I disturbed the hairstylist then. I have to go back home, it's too early to go to work. Maybe nobody's there yet. I'll try, I don't want to go back home, I'll go straight to work. I'll wait outside if nobody's around yet."

A car parked by the curb and shouted, "Hey."

Roberto recognized the hairstylist, "Oh hi, good morning."

Hairstylist Mhargie hopped out of the car and said, "What are you doing here, it's too early?

Roberto explained, "I forgot to get your contact number, but I remembered there was a phone number painted on the glass window. I thought I'd come back to get the number, that's why I'm here. You're early yourself."

Hairstylist Mhargie said, "I have an appointment, she's a nurse. She will be coming here from work. I thought I'd rather be here first—she might decide to go home if she sees that the salon is close."

Roberto said, "I have Thursdays off. My boss approved my request."

Hairstylist Mhargie said, "That's good, you can clean my house in the morning then you can go to

Julieta's after. You can schedule Olivia whenever you want. She's not important anyway."

Roberto was puzzled but did not further the questioning and said, "Ok."

Hairstylist Mhargie rummaged through the stuff in her pocketbook and said, "Oh before I forget, here's my number."

She handed Roberto her business card, Roberto politely took the card.

He asked, "Since Olivia is not important, I was wondering if you have Julieta's number, would you be able to give it to me?"

Hairstylist Mhargie said, "Oh yeah, her number is 555-123-4576. She usually picks up any call she gets. It will be easy for you to contact her. Here she is, my client is here. I have to open the salon now. See you Thursday, call me later or text me—I'll give you the address and the time you need to be there."

Roberto thanked her and rushed to take the bus back to work. He went to the small taxi office because the bus that just passed by his glance was the bus he needed to take to go to work. Taxi fare was a wallet hole-burner. He's not gonna do it again, he thought.

At noon, he called Julieta's number.

She said, "Hello. Who's this?"

Roberto replied, "Hi Julieta this is Roberto. Sorry to bother you. The hairstylist gave your number to me. I'd like to let you know that I got Thursday days-off. I can clean your house in the afternoon because the hairstylist wanted me to clean her apartment in the morning."

Julieta said, "That's great. I don't care what day, or what time as long as you can help me—I have no problem with that. So, it will be every Thursday afternoon?"

Roberto said, "Yes."

Julieta asked, "How about my sister Olivia? When can you schedule her?"

Roberto said, "I think I can make it during Wednesdays in the afternoon. But please don't tell your hairstylist that I have free time for your sister. I'd like to keep my schedule in tact that way—she might change her mind and tell me, she'd prefer Wednesdays instead of Thursdays. I have planned it to be that way already."

Julieta said, "You caught on very quickly. Mhargie is a piece of work—I tell yah."

Roberto said, "Ok Julieta, thank you very much. I have to go my boss is calling me."

Roberto tried to get the addresses of all the three ladies and their phone numbers. He received a text message.

Hairstylist Mhargie, "Here is the address, and I'd like for you to start at 10AM.

Roberto replied, "I think I need to start earlier, at 8AM is best. I'm not sure if I would have enough time to finish cleaning your apartment then go to Julieta's. I just think for my first day—10AM is too late. I need to figure out how to approach the work that I need to do in your apartment. I don't have any idea about the extent of work I need to do there. I hope it's ok with you."

Hairstylist Mhargie said, "Yeah, you're right. It makes sense, I'll just tell my boyfriend that you're coming at 8AM then. See you."

Roberto said, "Thanks."

CHAPTER ELEVEN

Working Hard

Roberto arrived at the apartment five minutes early. It was time consuming at first, he thought cleaning two houses in one day was too much. He didn't know what to do first and what to clean last. Hairstylist Mhargie left him by himself in the house, she cannot stay with him there—she's got clients to attend to. At 9AM, Larry, the boyfriend, left for work. He's an accountant—he had his own accounting firm in Jersey City. Roberto finished at 3PM. If Julieta's house was like that kind, maybe he can get done six hours tops. But not on the first day. He had to figure out how to do the job. He needed to commute from the hairstylist's apartment to Julieta's. He texted Julieta, she picked him up from the apartment to take him to her house.

Julieta said, "I told Mhargie, I am picking you up. I need to make sure you're in my house today so I'd know that my house is clean when I get home later tonight."

Roberto said, "Better yet, so I don't have to waste time waiting to catch the bus. I am tired from cleaning her apartment, the upstairs is a little bit hard. Not that I'm complaining, going up and down to clean is not easy. But I will get used to it I'm sure."

Julieta said, "I know, that's why a couple of house cleaners gave up on her already. Because of the going up and down the stairs. My house is easier to clean, trust me."

Roberto said, "Ok, I can't wait to see your house."

Julieta was just two blocks away from where Roberto's rooming house. Julieta was a block away from Landlady Josephine.

Roberto said, "This is where you live? This is your street? How come I've never seen you here? I walk to the laundromat every week taking these back roads and I haven't seen you until I met all of you in the hair salon? What a mystery that is?"

They went out of the car, Julieta let him in and said, "I don't usually stay here, I mean—I am at the office most of the time. I stay at Olivia's house until maybe 7PM after whatever time I get tired of office environment. I am with Olivia mostly and I mean mostly. I only work part time but I like hanging around the office or I'll be in the salon. My daughter works in Shorthills and goes to her boyfriend's house most of the time."

Roberto said, "Your house is better. I mean I can almost see everything from here. Not like her apartment, I was wondering what's upstairs and what's downstairs?"

Julieta said, "I have to go, my boss always needs me. Can't manage the office without me around. She can't answer any question without asking me first. You can have some apples if you want, there are oranges in the kitchen. You can grab a bottle of water in the pantry if you want. Help yourself, feel at home. Your money is on the fridge door, there's an envelope with a fridge magnet on top. If you finish six hours the money is worth six hours in the envelope. If you finish in five hours—it's all yours. But if you finish in seven hours, your loss. So, get done on time or less. All you have to do is lock all doors when you leave, that's all."

Roberto said, "Ok."

He thought it wasn't fair not to get paid the 7th hour if he finished the job in seven hours. But he's got to be able to find a way to finish in five hours. He knew where to get the cleaning stuff. The work he did from the apartment taught him what to do— fairly quickly. He looked for cleaning towels, there weren't any so he used the paper towels. He enjoyed cleaning Julieta's house more than the apartment. He finished in six hours, he was proud of himself. Julieta paid him for the day but the hairstylist didn't.

He texted Julieta, "I'm done. Thank you for the payment."

Olivia was using Julieta's phone replied, "Are you still at home?"

He replied, "I just got out of the house."

Olivia texted back, "Wait for us, we're already here at the laundromat. We're almost at the house."

He replied, "OK, I'll wait by the front door, I'll sit on the stoop."

The car pulled over, somebody from the passenger seat rolled the window down and waved.

Julieta was driving—Olivia hollered, "Roberto, we're here."

Roberto waived back and said, "I can see."

The car was parked on the street, Julieta said, "You did good, you got done on time."

Julieta handed the key to Olivia who then opened the door and said, "Let's go inside and eat."

Julieta said, "She cooked my favorite dish, Adobo. I want you to eat with us. You might be hungry."

Roberto said, "Oh no, I don't want to impose."

Olivia said, "You're not imposing. Oh, wow look at this house—finally cleaned and organized. Oh, look what you did with the remote controls. I don't even know where to pick up a remote control when I am here. Good job. It looked like you have housekeeping experience."

Roberto said, "Maybe what I did in the apartment this morning helped me to figure things out easier. And this is much better because everything is in one floor."

Olivia said, "Oh tell me about it. My house has a second floor. But I will make sure that you won't have a hard time. What I'll do is I'll dust a little bit here and there, I'll just make you vacuum, sweep, mop, take the garbage out and that's it. We'll work together don't worry."

Julieta said, "C'mon let's eat."

They were in the dining room. Roberto never had some kind of get together like this one ever since he moved to Union—five years and counting. He's by himself, all he did was go to work like the only purpose he had in life was go to work. He thought the sisters were kind hearted. He was celebrating in his heart that they appreciated his effort.

CHAPTER TWELVE

Caring For Family

After his work at the pizza store, he took the bus 66 going to Olivia's house. How convenient for him. There was a bus stop in front of the pizza store, just across the street that can take him to Olivia's.

Just like Olivia promised, they will work together. For his first time, she only asked him to clean the bathrooms—upstairs, one on the main floor and another in the basement. He only had to vacuum and mop the whole house. The last thing was to wash the dishes and clean up in the kitchen, the garbage was all out, that's it. He finished the work in four hours, he thought Olivia was right. The house was worth eight hours work. At least now he had an idea, next time he knew what to do. He knew he can get at it once he got going.

He went home exhausted, he tried to connect with his Mom online. He's learned that his sister's condition was getting worse. Her condition was contained at an early stage, but got aggressive. She got an open wound on her left foot, he's worried it might not heal.

He called his Mom, "Hello."

His Mom said, "Hello Roberto is that you?"

Roberto answered, "Yes it's me. How's Dad? How's Rizza?"

Mom said, "I've been keeping an eye on your sister's condition. Your Dad is eating well. He's been given showers by your Uncle Matt regularly. Rob can I request for Ginkgo Biloba supplement. And your Dad needs more diapers and sanitary wipes. Rizza needs insulin maintenance."

He said, "Mom I can't take care of Rizza's needs. I'll send money for her, so you can buy it there. I'll get yours and Dad's needs here and will ship it to you."

His Mom said, "Ok"

He took notes of all their requests. He's got to send a sea package again. With the part time job that he found maybe he can make a better budgeting plan this time. But he doesn't have time to shop, he can't do online orders because they might get a raise in rent again. He thought about what to do, he had a plan.

At the pizza store, he kept working hard and Boss Gerry couldn't be happier.

CHAPTER THIRTEEN

Old Flame

During his lunch break, Julieta entered the pizza store.

Julieta said, "Hey Roberto, fancy meeting you here. Finally, I notice you around here this time. Where's Gerry?"

Marlenny hollered, "Boss somebody's looking for you."

Boss Gerry walked to the front counter and said, "Of all the people, it's you."

Julieta said, "I just want a whole pie that's all. I'm not here to argue. I will if you want."

Boss Gerry said, "Marlenny take care of the order please."

Marlenny said, "Sure thing boss. Hey Julie, the usual?"

Julieta said, "Yes please. You know Roberto is a good house cleaner. I didn't know that he can help in the house."

Boss Gerry said, "Which house, your house?"

Julieta said, "Mine and Olivia and Mhargie."

Boss Gerry walked to where Roberto was having lunch and asked, "Is that true?"

Roberto asked, "What is it boss?"

Boss Gerry said, "You're housekeeping for her and her sister and the other one?"

Roberto said, "Hhhhmmm, aaaahhhh, yes boss."

Boss Gerry said, "And you didn't tell me?"

Roberto said, "What's the matter boss? I thought I'd do it on my day-off. I didn't think you would have a problem with it."

Boss Gerry said, "I don't, I am playing with you. I just didn't see you as a housekeeper."

Julieta walked close to the two after picking up her pie, "Is your boss giving you a hard time?"

Roberto said, "No, he was kidding around."

Boss Gerry said, "Hey Julie, you'd better take care of my guy. You know I'd kill anybody who'd mess up with him, right?

Julieta said, "Of course."

Boss Gerry said, "You know Roberto, she is the love of my life until she broke up with me. She thought I'd never want to take her daughter as mine, silly bitch. When are we going to get a civil wedding anyway, just like we planned?"

Julieta can only laugh, "Roberto how are you holding up?"

Roberto said, "I am thinking about the package for my Mom. My Dad needs this and that, the same goes for my sister."

Julieta said, "Why what's the problem."

Roberto said, "They're both sick, I need to send supplements and stuff.

Boss Gerry butted in, "His landlady will raise the rent again as soon as she sees that Roberto is buying stuff again. Those scumbags can't leave this guy alone. Now he's buying stuff for his sick Dad and they will think he has money to spare for another raise in rent. Greedy people."

Julieta said, "Let me see what I can do. Thanks Gerry. You know I still love you."

Boss Gerry said, "Yeah, yeah, yeah."

Roberto understood why Julieta would trust him, it's because Boss Gerry and her were an item before, that made sense. They had a past, he wondered—if it was off-again and on-again type thing.

CHAPTER FOURTEEN

Helping Hands

Julieta opened her detached garage. She gauged what stuff needed to be tossed and what's to be kept. She thought that Roberto would have to extend his hours beyond six. He needed an extra two hours to make space in the garage.

Julieta sent a text message to Roberto, she instructed him to clean the hairstylist's house in a jiffy the next time he's there. Of course, Roberto did what Julieta requested, he has closer business and friendly relationship with Julieta and Olivia through his boss.

Julieta appeared in the apartment, "Roberto are you done? Is Mhargie here?"

Roberto said, "No she's not here whenever I clean. I'm not done yet."

Julieta said, "What else do you need to do?"

Roberto said, "I will throw the garbage out, I only have five hours work here instead of six. I skipped her bedroom."

Julieta asked, "Why?"

Roberto said, "It's locked."

Julieta went upstairs and checked, "Why would she lock her bedroom, very odd. She wanted it cleaned every week, didn't she? That's her problem. Go throw the garbage out."

Roberto said, "I still have to stow the vacuum back in the closet and put plastic bags on the garbage bins."

Julieta said, "Hurry up so we can go to my house, I have a surprise for you."

He did not ask anymore. He just complied. He did the finishing touches in the apartment, locked the door and drove with Julieta. She showed him the garage.

She said, "If you can clean this part of the garage, you can put your box in there and complete your package for your family without your landlady bugging your ass."

Roberto jumped for joy, clapped his hands and said, "Oh my, thank you, thank you.

Julieta said, "You can clean up the house now, get it done as quickly as possible. You can extend two more hours for the garage if you need to. You can go home at 10PM later if that's ok with you. It's your call. The little space you can clean up in the garage is yours while you fix your package. This garage doesn't have a lock, just pull the handle up and continue to push upwards to open. Pull the handle down until it closes. But your box is safe, nobody steals anything from our garage."

Roberto couldn't imagine the kindness of Julieta. He wondered why she broke up with Boss Gerry. They would have been a perfect couple, no wonder everybody in the pizza store would say Boss Gerry only loved one woman and it was Julieta. Boss Gerry was married once, his wife died leaving him alone—without a child or children or a dog. But when Boss Gerry met Julieta, it was a different story. He loved Julieta like he never felt in love before. He had that deep affection for her that only Julieta can claw out of his heart.

CHAPTER FIFTEEN

Good Friends

Roberto still needed to figure out how to shop for his package, for the supplements and diapers it's easy. He needed to draft a good plan how to grab those open hours so he can do his errands. He came up with something, in the meantime he was scheming about Boss Gerry and Julieta.

At the pizza store, Roberto looked for Boss Gerry. He wasn't around yet. Marlenny had requested for Roberto to finish the pizza pans and he did.

Marlenny said, "That's why we love you here, you're always on top of your game."

Roberto said, "Thanks Marlenny, will it be alright if I talk to Boss Gerry when he comes in?"

Marlenny said, "Of course, I'm not his Mother you don't have to ask me permission. Certainly, I don't want to be his wife, otherwise my husband would have pulled me out of here a long time ago."

Roberto laughingly said, "Thanks."

He continued his work in the kitchen with anticipation. He can't stop thinking about what Julieta did for him. He was excited to tell Boss Gerry about it.

When Marlenny hollered. She said, "Roberto, boss is here."

Roberto went to the front counter and said, "Boss, Julieta helped me with the package. She asked me to clean the garage yesterday and she said I can use the space while I prepare the package for my family. I don't have to bring the stuff in the rooming, I can put it straight in the garage. She showed me how to open it and close it. I thought I'd let you know that she helped me solve the problem."

Boss Gerry said, "You did good kid. She's a great friend you know."

Marlenny said, "Yeah she's great and you let her go."

Boss Gerry said, "She broke up with me. What else can I do?"

Marlenny said, "Did you fight for your love for her? If you did, you know that you fought for the two of you not just yourself."

Boss Gerry said, "Too late now."

Roberto said, "It's never too late."

Boss Gerry said, "Look at you, I thought you're only interested in learning your job quickly."

They all laughed together and Roberto asked, "Boss I'd like to ask if I can give you some money that way when you go to Costso you can get some items for me to put in the package."

Boss Gerry said, "You want me to be your errand boy?"

They all laughed again and Roberto said, "I can go with you if you like. I can be here at the store before you leave for Costco."

Boss Gerry said, "And when would that be?"

Roberto said, "Whenever you need to go shopping and you schedule me to work at night. I can go with you in the morning and I can help you carry the stuff you bought."

Boss Gerry said, "Now we're talking. I will let you know, though I don't go there every week."

Roberto said, "It's ok boss. And maybe you can help me bring my stuff at Julieta's too."

Marlenny can't control her laughter and said, "You're on a roll Roberto. Bring it on, let the boss feel how it's like to be bossed around."

Roberto said with a chuckle, "Oh no boss. I think I can take it myself, don't worry. I'll do it on my own, I'll come up with something.

Boss Gerry said, "Certainly you won't bring Julieta here to pick up your stuff that we bought from Costo, right? You're not going to make me feel guilty, right?"

They all laughed.

CHAPTER SIXTEEN

Joy to Sorrow

He thought of his bosses—Gerry and Julieta made him remember his girlfriend when he was still living in Boundbrook.

They met when he was still working with the landscaping company. He liked working with lawnmowers, he thought his schooling was useful in quickly understanding how the machine worked. The problem was—he was not familiar about sloping grounds and gravity. He pushed the lawnmower up on a steep hill. He hit a gravity deficient spot. The lawnmower tipped over, he had an accident. He lost control, he fell and rolled on the ground, there was gravity where he fell. He had skin tear and deeply cut skin on his right arm.

His coworker thought of driving to the pharmacy close by. But his supervisor thought of bringing him to the urgent care—ReadyCare. His arm required medical care to stop the bleeding. Virginia was the receptionist, he was the patient. It wasn't a serious medical situation for him, he survived. But he wanted a serious situation with the receptionist. He was attracted to her, he went back there after a couple of weeks—to give her flowers as a thank you. She was gracious to him.

Virginia asked him, "How are you? I remembered you, you got scratched so bad—your skin won't stop bleeding."

Roberto said, "Yeah, you remembered."

Virginia said, "Of course I did. You're one of the most patient patient we have here."

SIDE COMMENT: Wait, do you call this an idiom—patient patient? No. But he's a patient who happened to have patience. Why didn't the writer wrote-it like that? Like what? You know you knew what I meant. Do I really have to explain it in detail?

Roberto asked, "Would it be alright if we can go for coffee or dessert sometime?"

Virginia said, "That's nice of you, we can go to the cafeteria right now. I'm done with my shift."

Roberto was stunned but can't refuse, "Sure. Let's go, lead the way."

Virginia said, "This way."

They ordered hot coffee and dessert. They weren't in the cold season yet but they ordered hot coffee. They talked for an hour exchanged numbers and she headed her way. Roberto had to wait for his coworker to get done with his errands before they can both go home. His friend picked him up—he was Roberto's ride.

Roberto and Virginia called each other, texted, dated and had fun together. Roberto never had this much fun before, she always picked him up. She drove a Toyota Corolla while Roberto can't drive. He felt like the whole world was perfect in the midst of its imperfection.

When winter time came—one morning Virginia was on her way to work, the temperature dropped. From her apartment to her job—it was only a distance of almost eight miles. She was a defensive driver, she followed road courtesy, doesn't want to get a ticket, doesn't want to get involved in any accident, don't want for others to get hurt.

She was approaching the railroad underpass. She hit a patch of black ice, her car slid. She tried to control the car, she panicked seeing the concrete block wall of the underpass, she lost her grip. It was a fatal crash, she didn't make it to the hospital.

Roberto received a broadcast text message from Virginia's phone.

It was her mother.

> "To all of Virginia's friends. I regret
> to be the bearer of a very sad news. My
> daughter passed away this morning due to
> a car crash in the Edison train underpass.
> My heart is grieving—I did not want for
> all of you to grieve too. But I have to
> let you all know what happened to her. I
> will miss her and I believe you will all
> miss her too. Thank you very much for your
> friendship with my daughter. I will cherish
> her memories as long as I live."

Roberto can't believe what happened to Virginia. Why Virginia? They had been together for three years, they've been talking about getting married even if they did not get engaged yet. They were planning a family, she wanted five boys. Roberto agreed with her, although he knew they might have girls somewhere in that five. She was very understanding and loving, even if she knew he was out of status—she accepted him. She was willing to dream big with him and would stop at nothing to achieve them. They wanted to settle in Pennsylvania—in Morgantown, or East Earl or Ephrata. They thought it's better there, the environment was restful compared to Edison or Boundbrook. They visited those places whenever they had chances to go out of state. They both liked Rockvale Outlets and Tanger Mall. He bought a necklace for himself and for Virginia at QVC in Rockvale.

He did not look at her as the ticket to his coveted green card. He loved her, with all of his heart. She was 25, he was 26. A persistent thought kept running through his mind—who and what would be his inspiration now that she's gone? How would he move forward? Could he still dream dreams? Could he still make plans? What was the purpose of his life now?

Roberto was devastated—hurting very badly. He doesn't know if he can go back to work to function properly. But he still found purpose when he called his family in his country.

Roberto dialed his Mom's landline, "Hello Mom."

His sister answered the phone, "This is Kristina, Roberto is that you? Mom its Roberto. It is Roberto, hurry up. Mom is in the kitchen, I am keeping Dad company here in the living room. How are you?"

Roberto said, "I'm ok, how's Dad?"

Kristina said, "He's ok, of course he's not getting any better. We know that the doctor said he only has 10 years to live. Let's hope for more."

Roberto asked, "How are you? Is Rizza following doctor's orders?"

Roberto's Mom took the handset, "Hello my son, how are you? Your Dad is here watching TV in the living room."

Roberto's voice started to crack, "Mom Virginia died in a car crash. I don't know what to do."

His Mom cried, "Oh my god, no, no, oh my god. When did it happen? How did it happen? How are you? How's her family? Are you ok? Do you want to take a vacation or an extra day-off, or a one-week off or something?

Kristina was crying too, she asked, "Mom what happened? Why are you crying? Is Roberto ok, immigration got him?"

Mom said, "No, Virginia died in a car crash."

Kristina walked away, she doesn't want Roberto to hear her cry. But Roberto could hear her sobbing on the phone from afar. They couldn't say anything anymore, they were just crying on the phone. They all decided to just hung up for there were no words to express their grief for what happened. What's next? What now? Nobody knew the answer.

Roberto kept in his mind what Kristina said that day. He remembered his Dad wasn't getting any better. He mustered to go back to work. He'd like to do whatever it takes to support his Dad, now more than ever before. He lost Virginia, he won't allow for anything to happen to Rizza and his Dad this time. How can he handle losing the people he loved, so he thought?

CHAPTER SEVENTEEN

Continuing Courtesy

He's been dedicated to his job at the pizza store. His housekeeping job got more demanding. One day when Roberto was cleaning the apartment the hairstylist talked to him about her plan.

Hairstylist Mhargie, "Roberto I need help in the salon, you need to clean it for me. I cannot hire another person, because I don't know who to trust."

He said, "I can't do the salon, but I will try to squeeze it in my schedule if I can. I can't promise you but I will try. Maybe you can find someone else. You didn't trust me either at first."

Hairstylist Mhargie said, "I don't want to waste my time looking for another housekeeper."

Roberto can only say, "I will really try, but I can't promise."

After the apartment Roberto went straight to Julieta's house. Nobody was available to pick him up that day. He took the bus 114 from NY going to Bridgewater. He got out from the bus in front of the laundromat and walked ten minutes to Julieta's house. He has his own key, Julieta gave him a copy just in case nobody can let him in the house. It was already 8PM when Julieta got home.

As soon as she opened the front door—she said, "Hi Roberto, are you in the kitchen?"

Roberto said, "Yes, I didn't hear you open the door. I was trying to hurry up so that I can fix the box afterwards."

She said, "Do you still need to buy some stuff to fill in your package box?"

Roberto said, "Yes. But I only need a couple bags of gummy candies. My brother loves them. Julieta, I have a problem. Your hairstylist required me to clean the salon. Next time I need to clean your house—I can be here around 6PM. I'll schedule the cleaning for the living room, bathroom, kitchen and the dining room. I'll clean the bedrooms a day ahead. I think I can work it out that way. But please don't tell the hairstylist about my plans."

Julieta said, "We can go to Walmart if you want, it closes midnight, we have time."

Roberto said, "Ok, I'll finish up."

Julieta said. "I knew Mhargie's gonna do that to you. Ok here's what I can do to help you. You've got to call me as soon as you get done in the salon. That way I have an idea when to pick you up if I can. I am assuming that you can clean the salon for two hours. If she does not agree on the two hours that you propose, I will talk to her. I need your help too—she cannot deny me that. I will still pick you up to make sure you'll clean my house. I'll ask my sister to pick you up if I can't. You know if my sister and I won't do that—Mhargie will keep you working. But if she sees that I am around she will be happy with whatever you can contribute to the salon. That bitch will wear you out, she thinks she owns you. Do you understand what I'm saying?"

Roberto said, "Yeah I understand what you're saying. Sometimes she wanted me to mow the lawn—it's pretty small but I'm not mowing it. She needs a landscaper to deal with the lawn or the yard or the fences or whatever. I'm just a house cleaner, I can't be paid as a house cleaner and then do landscaping job. Plus, she's taking so much of my time—I need to clean your house too."

Roberto finally finished up—they both hopped in the car headed to Walmart. Roberto bought more than the gummy candies he thought were the only ones he needed. He remembered his brother—he loved hot chocolates with marshmallows in them. His oldest sister loved the honey roasted peanuts and his Mom loved the pecan shortbread cookies.

Julieta said, "Keep the stuff that you bought in the car. Next week when you come back to clean the house remind me to take the stuff out so you can fill the box. Are you almost ready to close it?"

Roberto said, "Almost."

Julieta said, "Ok good. I'll see you next week, good night."

CHAPTER EIGHTEEN

Fanning the Embers

Days passed by, the pizza store was busy during lunch time. Roberto needed to talk to Boss Gerry about the last item he needed from Costco. He wrote a note and gave it to Marlenny then went back to the kitchen.

She said, "Hey boss, this is the last item that the boy needed for his box. I'll tell him you're not going to Costco for two weeks, but go there anyway and get this for him. I'd like for you to get this box of chocolates for his family in my behalf. He's been a good kid. He worked tirelessly, he deserved a break."

Boss Gerry said, "Good thinking."

Roberto asked Marlenny, "Is he available?"

Marlenny said, "He's busy. I think he's not going there for two weeks. But I made sure he got your message."

Roberto said, "Ok, thanks."

Marlenny said, "Do you have housekeeping later?"

Roberto said, "Yes, it's Olivia's turn tonight."

Marlenny said, "Ok, I know where she lives. What time do you finish work there?"

Roberto said, "It's an 8-hour job, I might be done 10PM."

Marlenny said, "Much better, text me as soon as you're done at Olivia's later."

Roberto said, "Why?"

Marlenny said, "Just text me."

Olivia did some light cleaning as usual. She dusted the piano, watered the indoor plants and wiped the dripped water on the floor. She dusted the TV and polished the coffee table. She didn't want Roberto to clean the bedroom at the main floor. She had her tax papers and other documents in there so she doesn't want the bedroom bothered. Roberto was happy but needed to text Marlenny as soon as he's done, hoping he won't forget. He finished cleaning at 9PM instead of 10PM, he texted Marlenny.

Marlenny texted back, "Ok, the boss is on his way to pick you up."

Roberto said, "Why?"

Marlenny replied, "Boss will take you back to Julieta's so you can close the package. He also got the box of chocolates you wrote on the note. I asked him to get it for you."

Roberto exclaimed and texted the word, "Wow!"

Olivia asked, "Roberto what's the matter? Are you ok?"

Roberto said, "Oh yes Olivia. My boss will pick me up here right now. He will take me to Julieta's house. He's bringing the box of chocolates that I wanted for my nieces and nephews. We will head to Julieta's so I can put the box in the garage."

Olivia said, "I thought something happened to you. Ok let's wait in the living room until he comes."

Roberto said, "Thank you Olivia, at least I finish at 9PM today."

It didn't take long when they saw the headlights of a car heading for Olivia's drive way. She opened the door, but kept the storm door closed. Roberto was sitting on the couch which was pushed back to rest against the wall where a french window was resting atop. He turned to look outside from the window, they both recognized Boss Gerry's car. Roberto hurriedly got out of the house, for it was already late. He bid goodbye to Olivia and she handed him a small white envelope, his money was inside it.

Olivia said, "Say hi to Gerry for me."

Roberto said, "Will do and thanks again."

Boss Gerry parked in front of the detached garage at Julieta's house. Roberto knocked on the front car-door while Boss Gerry waited inside his car. The car-doors unlocked, Roberto opened the back door, threw his stuff in then jumped in the passenger seat.

Julieta was watching TV in her bedroom room when Roberto finally decided to ring the doorbell since there was no attention given to his knocking. Julieta jumped off her bed wondering who was at the door. She thought it might be Olivia bringing her some cold cuts again from Shoprite. Or it might have been Dana, too tired to drive home at Alwyn's house in Edison. She peeked at the door peephole to check who was outside.

She opened the door and said, "Oh my god Roberto, what are you doing here?"

Roberto said, "I need to close the box, Boss Gerry drove me here. He's in the car in front of the garage. Can he come in, while he waits for me?"

Julieta said, "Yes, of course. Call him, tell him to come in. I'll make some lemonade in the kitchen. I'll turn the TV on in the living room so he can watch Indiana Jones."

Roberto said while walking in Boss Gerry's direction, "Ok."

He knocked on the car window. It rolled down, "Boss, Julieta said you can come in, while you wait for me."

Boss Gerry said, "Ok, how long do you think you'll finish up the box?"

Roberto said, "I'll finish up in less than an hour."

Boss Gerry said, "Take your time but don't take too long. We have work tomorrow."

Roberto said, "Ok, boss."

Boss Gerry handed Roberto the box of chocolates, he headed to the garage.

Boss Gerry walked to the front door. It has been a long time since he waited to spend some time with Julieta again—spend time with her alone. He sort of wanted this thing to happen—he missed her. He wanted so badly to talk to her, the two of them together in the kitchen chatting or in the living room flipping through channels from YouTube. He thought this is can be a perfect night.

Roberto opened the garage door and turned the light on. He saw the stuff that he bought from Walmart, Julieta brought it in the garage. Julieta's gesture made it easy for Roberto to arrange the stuff in and then close up the box.

Boss Gerry knocked on the door, Julieta answered and said, "Come in."

Boss Gerry said, "Hi, I hope I'm not imposing. I just want to make sure for him to finish up the box so he can send it soon."

Julieta said, "No imposition at all. I'd love to help him too. And you're always welcome here, you know that. Or you have forgotten about it?"

Boss Gerry said, "In that case I will visit more often."

Julieta said, "I'd love that. Do you want some iced tea, or coffee, I have some lemonade?"

Boss Gerry said, "I'll have a glass of lemonade, I'd like to chill and watch TV with you. Is that ok?"

Julieta said, "Of course, anytime."

Julieta and Boss Gerry chatted the time away. He didn't care about what channel it was or what show it was. He gave his undivided attention to Julieta. He enjoyed every minute of it.

Roberto was done fixing the box, but he wanted for the two to spend more time together. He closed the garage door, and slept inside the car. An hour passed by, Boss Gerry and Julieta were still having a good time chatting when she checked the time. It was already midnight.

Julieta said, "Gerry you better check on the boy, it's midnight he must be done already."

Boss Gerry said, "Ok, thanks for a lovely night. If he's done I will take him home. If not, I will still take him home. Will it be alright with you if I come back again sometime?"

Julieta said, "Of course, I enjoyed tonight with you."

Boss Gerry said, "Is tomorrow too soon?"

Julieta said, "I will see what's going on in the office. I'll check with Olivia's activities—if she doesn't need me, I will let you know. Do you still have the same number, if not I can call the pizza store?"

Boss Gerry said, "Yes I do, I'll wait for your call. I will check on the boy, good night and thanks again."

Boss Gerry found Roberto sleeping in the car. He let him sleep, started the car and drove him home. He needed to go to sleep so the only thing he'll worry about will be the package pick-up the following day. In the meantime, Boss Gerry had to take his beauty rest because he needed to be at the store early in the morning for inventory and prep.

CHAPTER NINETEEN

Bitter Accusation

Roberto called the shipper and scheduled a pick up. He made sure that the pick-up day would be the same when he's scheduled to clean Julieta's house. While he was still in the pizza store that day, Marlenny asked about the update on his package.

She said, "Hey Roberto, how are you? How's the package going? How's the boss?"

Roberto said, "Oh, Marlenny. Thank you so much for the chocolates. My nieces and nephews will love them. Thanks so much. I finished packing, I closed the box and called the shipper to pick it up during my schedule to clean Julieta's house, I got the schedule."

Marlenny asked, "When will that be?"

Roberto said, "Sometime next week. Thursday around 7PM."

Marlenny asked, "Is Julieta gonna be home?"

Roberto said, "She goes home in different hours, sometimes 7PM sometimes 8PM. But for sure 8PM she's in the house. Why?"

Marlenny said, "Just asking, you know—the boss was there when you closed the package. And I bet he enjoyed keeping you company."

Roberto said, "No, he went inside the house. He cannot possibly watch me tape my package, that's silly. He spent time with Julieta. Oh, I get what you're saying. I'll ask Julieta to be home at 8PM, if she asks why—I'll make up a story. You're in charge of the boss, going to Julieta's. That's not my assignment—that's yours. Oh men, how I wish they were married."

Marlenny said, "Now you're talking."

Roberto hadn't missed any schedule at the pizza store. He was busy this time more than before and he got tired often more than before. The staff in the pizza store can see it—but he still pushed to give his best.

He was cleaning the hairstylist's apartment. She got so hysterical and accused Roberto of stealing.

She said, "Roberto, I have given you a chance. I trusted you upon the recommendations of my friends. I lost the envelope that I placed on top of the hanging wall shelf in the living room. A white envelope containing $1,800 rent money. The landlord requested for cash payment this month because there are repairs that need to be done in the house. I welcomed you here and you stole money from me?"

Roberto said, "I don't know what you're talking about. I did not see any envelope anywhere. Which hanging shelf did you put it on and when did you put it there?"

Hairstylist Mhargie said, "Fred will collect it today. I told him yesterday that it was ready, he can pick it up anytime. He would have texted or called me if he picked it up, he never did."

Roberto panicked he called Julieta and said, "Please help me. I am at your hairstylist's apartment. Her money is missing, she said I stole it. I didn't steal anything. Please help me, she might call the police. I don't want that to happen to me."

Julieta as always—picked up the call talked softly and said, "Roberto, calm down. I will call her. I am in a meeting right now. But I will call her, I will text Olivia to go there and check out the situation. She has a lot of time in her hands—that's what retired people have in abundance."

Roberto said, "Please help me, please hurry up."

Julieta texted her sister, "Olivia whatever it is that you're doing—please drop it and go to Mhargie's apartment. Hurry up please—Roberto is in trouble I think, Mhargie is accusing him of stealing money."

Olivia was ready to go out of the house to do food shopping. She closed the front door, when she heard her phone beeped in her pocketbook. She stood on the third of the four steps at the front door and looked at her phone. She saw a text message, it was from Julieta. She hurriedly went to her car upon reading it then drove to the apartment. She was on the landing of the hairstylist's front door when she saw the landlord parking his car on the street. She left the door and waited for Fred to park, she walked to his car and knocked on the window.

Fred rolled the window down and said, "Good morning Olivia."

Olivia said, "Good morning Fred, how are you?"

Fred said, "What can I do for you, my lady?"

Olivia said, "Fred were both senior citizens now. I think I can ask you a straight question."

Fred said, "Oh my, I am loving your direct approach. What's the matter?"

Olivia said, "Do you have time to go out on a date with me?"

Fred said, "You make me blush Olivia, you know that I wanted to go out with you a long time ago. I just didn't have the chance to ask you. But I love the idea of you and me going out on a date."

Olivia said, "Come on, let's go, come with me."

Fred said, "Where? It's too early."

Olivia said, "Come with me in Mhargie's apartment."

They both walked to the front door. She rang the doorbell, Roberto opened the door.

Olivia asked, "How are you? Come on Fred let's go inside."

Fred asked, "Where's Mhargie?"

Olivia asked the same question, "Where's Mhargie?"

Hairstylist Mhargie heard the voices in the living room and said, "Roberto what are you doing?"

Roberto went to the office—stood near by the door and said, "Olivia is here, with a guy."

Hairstylist Mhargie, "Who's guy?"

Roberto said, "I don't know him."

Hairstylist Mhargie walked out of the office and said, "Oh my god Fred. I had the rent money ready since yesterday when we spoke on the phone. I can't find the envelope that I put on the hanging wall shelf and now it's gone. There's nobody here in this house but the cleaner and me—and the envelope is gone. I don't know what to do. I am trying to help him, gave him a part time job and this is what I get. The money was stolen."

Olivia said, "You cannot accuse him of something like that."

Fred said, "I agree with Olivia, because yesterday when we talked on the phone you said that the envelope was on the hanging wall shelf. You're in Jersey City, that's what you said. You know that I am going to get the money—and when I have it I usually inform you. Well I got the money I just forgot to inform you. So, nobody stole anything from anyone."

Hairstylist Mhargie, "Oh my god, Fred. I was worried sick about where did the money go and where am I going to get another $1,800 to give you."

Fred said, "I'm sorry I forgot, but you can't assume that this boy stole it. He's been your housekeeper for a while now. Although he doesn't know me, I know he's been your employee for quite some time now. If he did not steal anything from you from the start it is most likely he will not steal from you at all. Plus, he works for Gerry, you of all people should know that when a person works for Gerry and stays with Gerry for a year or two or more. That person can be trusted."

Olivia asked, "Roberto are you done cleaning? Hey, Mhargie I went here because Julieta asked me to check the situation. If Roberto stole the money, he would have had an earful from me. But he clearly did not."

Hairstylist Mhargie, "I was just worried."

Roberto was relieved when he heard what happened and said, "I am almost done. I have the kitchen to clean and the living room, that's it."

Olivia bid Mhargie goodbye. She went out of the apartment and headed to the grocery store to do her food shopping. Fred was left behind, he spoke to Mhargie some more—discussing the requirements of the repairs. The kitchen needed updating, a new set of washer and dryer needed to be installed. And most importantly the roof and sidings needed changing.

Olivia texted Roberto, "Are you done, with Mhargie's?"

Roberto said, "Yes, I am walking to the bus stop now."

Olivia said, "Stop walking, are you close to the apartment yet?"

Roberto said, "Yes, ten steps away."

Olivia said, "Ok, stay there. Where ever that ten steps is, I'll come and get you."

Roberto said, "Thank you, thanks very much."

Olivia drove Roberto to Julieta's house to clean.

She asked, "Aren't you going to clean the salon?"

Roberto said, "No, not anymore. I'm done with her. I talked to her in front of Fred that I cannot do house cleaning for her anymore. I'm not cleaning the salon either. What happened today scared the shit out of me. This is the first time in my life that I have been accused of stealing. And I didn't know how to handle it. I wanted to cry, but I can't. It was frustration and confusion and stress all at the same time. I am not having it anymore, besides the fact that she pays me late all the time. Sometimes she forgets and I have to remind her that she didn't pay me yet. And I would have to explain to her—this payment was for this date and the other one was for a week ago and for today there's no payment yet. All those things became an added load on my shoulders."

Olivia said, "Oh my god, I didn't know she's been doing that to you on a regular basis. I had a hunch she will do it once or twice but not this often. I'll tell Julieta what happened, ok?"

Roberto said, "Ok. I'll start cleaning."

CHAPTER TWENTY

Lovers Again

Roberto was early in Julieta's house. He skipped the salon, it would mean he will get done early. He was supposed to be at Julieta's until maybe 10PM or a little later.

He called the pizza store he knew Marlenny will pick up, "Hey, I am going to get done here early."

Marlenny said, "Roberto? Where early? What early?"

Roberto said, "This is Roberto, Marlenny. I will finish early at Julieta's."

Marlenny said, "Then finish early, just watch TV when you're done. Feel at home, you're at home in that house anyway. Plus, you have to wait for the package to be picked up."

Roberto said, "Oh shit, I forgot about that. I didn't have enough money. I'll finish early, now I have to really finish early. I'll walk back to the house and get extra $20 and then go back here. Ok, bye Marlenny."

Marlenny said, "Roberto wait, don't forget about our deal tonight."

Roberto asked, "What deal?"

Marlenny said, "Boss was supposed to be at Julieta's at 8PM. They will spend the night together watching TV again."

Roberto asked, "And what was the reason why he needed to be here?"

Marlenny said, "I told boss you requested him to help you with the package, when there's no package. As soon as your package got picked up—the shipper will give you a new box, right? I told boss he needed to pick you up because you wanted to go to Walmart. Julieta cannot take you to Walmart tonight. He got mad, but I reminded him that you deserve all the help that he can give you. Because you do more than what's expected of you. He cannot do anything but agree."

Roberto said, "So I just have to wait for him—or them?"

Marlenny said, "Yes sir."

Roberto finished the cleaning at Julieta's house early as expected. He took the $20 from home, he didn't care if Gemma was watching or not.

Back at Julieta's house—he watched TV and chill in the living room. Julieta went home early to talk to Roberto about what happened.

Julieta said, "I'll talk to Mhargie tomorrow. Olivia gave me the details about the stealing incident. That bitch will never change, I tell yah. She's been like that even before you met us."

Roberto looked at the time it was 6:45PM. He said, "Julieta I have to go to the garage and wait for the shipper, my package will be picked up tonight at 7PM. I gave instructions to the driver where to park."

Julieta said, "Go. Come back when it's all done."

The shipper arrived fifteen minutes late. Roberto did all the paper works and the package was set. He was elated that his Dad's needs will at least be addressed somehow. He can't do everything all at once but he's determined to give support for his family. He saw Boss Gerry's car, he waved at him from the garage door. Boss Gerry parked his car and rolled the window down.

He hollered, "Come on, let's go to Walmart."

Roberto said, "What Walmart boss?"

Boss Gerry said, "Marlenny said you need a ride to Walmart tonight. I was so pissed, I'm tired."

Roberto said, "Don't worry about Walmart boss, why don't we chill inside."

Boss Gerry said, "Inside where? In the garage?"

Roberto said, "No boss, inside the house."

Boss Gerry asked, "Who's house? What house?"

Robert said, "Come on boss, Julieta is inside. She's making something for dinner. Why don't you go in and I'll clean up the garage for a little bit?"

Boss Gerry asked, "She's home?"

Roberto said, "Yes boss. The door is open, knock and you can open it yourself."

Boss Gerry said, "Yeah, but she's not expecting me."

Roberto said, "She kinda expected that when I'm around here—you're around too. Let's go I'll let you in."

Boss Gerry was comforted to learn that Julieta was home. They both walked to the door. Roberto knocked and turn the door knob and opened the door.

He said, "Julieta—I come bearing a gift."

Julieta said, "Oh Gerry, come in. I didn't expect you."

Boss Gerry said, "That's what I just said."

Julieta said, "No but come in. I'm glad you're here. I made some dinner, I thought the boy had not eaten yet. I didn't realize he already ate. Would you like to have some? He was here early because of what happened to him at the apartment."

Boss Gerry asked, "What happened?"

Roberto said, "Julieta I'll just go back to the garage. I'll put away some stuff, I don't really want to hear any more of the incident."

Julieta said, "Ok, go. Bring some food with you if you like. Or hurry up with whatever you need to do at the garage and come back here. Don't sleep in the car again."

Boss Gerry asked, "What incident? What did you do?"

Julieta said, "He didn't do anything but clean the apartment, that's all."

Roberto went in the kitchen, he took a paper plate and plastic spoon and fork. He walked out of the house, went in the garage. Julieta explained to Boss Gerry what happened.

Julieta said, "He's not going to clean the apartment anymore, not the salon either. I can't blame him, he kept putting up with Mhargie. She's abusive. He lost that part of his income but I say it's a god riddance."

Boss Gerry said, "I can't believe he had to go through that stress with what's going on with his family and his living conditions with a witch landlady. I'm surprised he still can get up in the morning and go to work. Mhargie is really a piece of work. By the way, when are we going to the city hall for our civil wedding?"

Julieta said, "That's what I told him, Mhargie is a real ass. Civil wedding you said? You've got to be kidding me."

Roberto slept in the car again. Boss Gerry and Julieta realized that they were enjoying themselves and forgot the time. This time they both talked about being together again. Boss Gerry can schedule to be at Julieta's and Julieta can do the same in Boss Gerry's place. It was great news and Marlenny would be over the moon with the progress.

CHAPTER TWENTY-ONE

Familial Struggles

When Boss Gerry dropped him off at home by midnight Roberto allotted ten minutes to talk to his Mom.

He said, "Mom, the box got picked up already."

His brother was the one who picked up the call. "It's Kevin."

Roberto said, "Hey Kev, how's everybody?"

Kevin cried and said, "Dad's the same, Rizza is kind of having a situation. She got an open wound on her left foot. It has been an open wound for some time now. Mom didn't want to tell you, she doesn't want you to worry. I'm scared for her and for Dad, sometimes my chest is aching I don't know what to do."

Roberto said, "Stop crying Kev, Mom might see you. Did Rizza go to the doctor?"

Kevin said, "Yes, the doctor gave her some medications. But there's no assurance. It might not take long, if the wound doesn't heal—she will end up losing her foot. That's what the doctor said.

Kevin controlled himself—his Mom saw him on the phone and asked, "Is that Roberto you're talking to?"

Kevin said, "Yes Mom."

His Mom took the handset and said, "How are you doing?"

Roberto said, "Don't worry about me, how's Dad? The box finally got picked up. Its ninety days wait, you are aware of that, right?"

Mom said, "Yeah, I know."

Roberto said, "I quit cleaning the apartment, the owner accused me of stealing. I am ok, my boss from the house that I'm cleaning backed me up. I still have my job at the pizza store—though my boss got pissed, he got over it right away. He's got a girlfriend now. Mom, whatever is going on with Rizza you know I still can help you right? I will keep on budgeting my salary, I stopped buying shirts now. I don't want my landlady to think that I got extra money to spend on shirts. I'll give them all to you after I've paid all my bills the rest is yours."

Mom cried and said, "Thank you so much. You've been a big help to all of us. But don't forget yourself, it's also important that you take care of yourself."

Roberto said, "I know Mom, I just thank the LORD I have my boss helping me. And the sisters are helping me too. Mom, I have to go. I need to go to work tomorrow. I'd like to talk some more, it's already passed midnight over here."

Mom said, "Ok, goodnight then. Don't deprive yourself of sleep, you need it. Don't work too hard, you might get worn out before you know it."

Roberto said, "Goodnight Mom."

CHAPTER TWENTY-TWO

Occurring Errors

He had trouble at the pizza store, life wasn't perfect after all. Mistakes were around when you don't need them, but that's how life goes. Boss Gerry don't mind, Marlenny don't mind.

Boss Gerry hollered, "Be careful there. We will end up using SOLO cups if drinking glasses keep breaking."

Marlenny hollered, "Whoever broke the glass, don't listen to him. We all know that's part of business."

They all laughed, the other staff don't mind—they only got reminded that they too made mistakes in their lives. Roberto would drop a drinking glass and would break. Of course, everybody knew that it's part of the overhead expenses, but of course they were always careful not to repeat the same mistakes—even in life. The problem was—in case of glass breakages or spills, there'd always be additional work to do.

Boss Gerry received visits from Julieta at the pizza store pretty regularly. Marlenny was loving every minute of it.

CHAPTER TWENTY-THREE

Still Hoping

Roberto got used to having time due to him losing the apartment job. While he got the two houses to clean he called his Mom almost every week. Roberto heard the phone on the other line ringing.

It was picked up by his Mom, "Hello."

Roberto said, "Mom, it's me."

She cried, "Rizza's foot got amputated. The doctor said—it's better that way. We can't wait for it to get better or to heal. Rather than get serious infection, it was better to cut it off. Oh my god Roberto, I didn't mean to bring this news to you now."

Roberto said, "Stop crying Mom. We cannot do anything about it anymore."

Roberto was crying, he cursed, he almost shouted. He heard a knock on his bedroom door.

He said, "Mom I will call you back in five minutes, I think it's Ronald knocking on my door."

His Mom said, "Ok."

Roberto opened the door and said, "Hey Ronald, what's up man?"

Ronald asked, "How are you man? Is everything ok? I heard you curse pretty loudly."

Roberto said, "I was talking to my Mom. My sister was sick, we thought she will get better. But she's diabetic—her foot got amputated. I didn't even know it was already that bad. I thought she just had trouble from an open wound that took time to heal. I never realized that it won't really heal until her foot got cut off."

Ronald said, "I'm sorry man. I'm not really good at words and I hope you won't get offended, but in my mind at least she's still alive you know. Maybe the doctors or the people around her can still help her reduce the total risk of her condition you know."

Roberto said, "I can only hope. I cannot do anything more, I tried. But I can't stop now."

Ronald said, "Well you've got to take care of yourself too, you know. If you falter they're affected. You've got to understand that even machines break down sometimes, we can get sick too—but don't you get sick. Because you keep your family going, so better take care of yourself. Set this as an example, your family have diabetes so you would know what to do not to get it. They say it's genetics, lifestyle, and food, etcetera. I don't know what's the truth about it but the main thing is, you've got to be able to find time to rest. You need to breath."

Roberto said, "Thanks man, I appreciate it."

Ronald said, "Before I forget, I met a girl—we're dating but not a steady one yet. We're working on it though."

Roberto said, "I'm happy for you man, congrats. At least one of us is happy. I can't wait to get out of this shit hole."

They both went back into their recluse. Roberto didn't know anything else but work. He tried to enjoy life but could only do so much. Living life and having a life costs money. It doesn't come free of charge.

The constant dating of Boss Gerry and Julieta was a serious path for them to now have been engaged. Fred and Olivia started going out. Roberto only knew that the hairstylist was looking for another housekeeper other than that he doesn't know anything about her. He doesn't ask, he doesn't care, he don't give a damn.

A couple of weeks passed when Roberto got a chance to call his Mom again.

She picked up the phone, "Hello, who is this?"

Roberto answered, "It's me, Mom."

His Mom can't control herself, she cried, "Your sister, Roberto."

Roberto asked, "Who Mom, I have three of them alive?"

Mom said, "Rizza, her leg got amputated, she's not getting better. She's been suffering from gangrene the doctor did not have any more options. Oh my god, I don't understand what's going on in our family."

Roberto cried, "Mom I think I need to take the chance to write a letter to USCIS now. I can't wait for anymore disaster to happen to our family. Don't worry of what's going to happen. I need to try Mom. I have been in this country for a long time, I have to do something. I will use the petition case that was filed for you by Aunt Paula. I've got to be able to get something out of those papers, I am a derivative somehow. I will see what I can do. Maybe we can all get together here in this country one of these days. Right Mom?"

Mom said, "Just do whatever you can, and be careful all the time my son."

Roberto said, "Don't worry Mom."

Roberto sat at the edge of the bed, he's mind was running a mile a minute with thoughts that he doesn't know he understood—questions he doesn't know the answers. He rummaged through his stuff looking for his documents folder. He found the petition paper of Aunt Paula in behalf of his Mom. He doesn't know where Aunt Paula was. She had stopped calling his Mom and wrote a Christmas card only twice in her lifetime from California. My Mom understood her sister's situation in the US. People are always busy if they're not working—it's either their looking for a second job or looking for a third job. His Mom told him about Aunt Paula's busy life. Roberto understood it—because he himself ended up having two jobs, and still not enough.

He searched through the internet on what to do, he cannot find any answers for himself as far as using the petition papers were concerned. He went to different immigration lawyers. The lawyers don't have any answers for him. He was only advised to get married to a US citizen. If there was no way to get married—then somebody has got to file a sponsorship for him. That was the easy way he can get himself into—he can get petitioned and he can get a green card eventually. He finally drafted a letter.

May 16, 2021

To whom it may concern:

I am submitting this letter including an application form I-698 in the interest of obtaining a legal status here in the United States. I have attached the petition papers that was filed on my mother's behalf in which I am a derivative of the said petition. Please consider reviewing the application and the documents that I have submitted.

I called the USCIS office last April 2021, but I was only advised to consult a lawyer. I have consulted more than four lawyers before. I was only advised to get married.

I would appreciate any information you can give me about the application. Thank you very much for your kind consideration on this matter.

Very truly yours,

Roberto David

He went to the post office to buy the money order to pay for the hefty application fee of $1,755 for I-698.

He mailed it. It was weeks after he received the packet from USCIS—his application was returned to him. He was not able to tick the box in the application specifying that his home address and mailing address in the US were the same.

CHAPTER TWENTY-FOUR

Overstepping

One morning he was about to go to work, he was washing the dishes in the sink and Ronald went out of his bedroom. They almost struck a conversation when Landlady Josephine opened the door of their flat—the "attic."

She said, "I was checking the mailbox downstairs. I opened this mail because I cannot see the name of the addressee from the window of the envelope. It's for you Roberto. Congratulations, now you can look at a brighter future."

Roberto without any emotion can only say, "Thank you."

Ronald waited for Landlady Josephine to disappear and said, "What the flipping hell was that? She looks and thinks at you like you're not human because you don't have a green card. She operates an illegal rooming house and opens the letter that does not belong to her. Doesn't she know who will get immigration letters here. No offense my friend, but it's only you. You're the only one right now who's doing business with USCIS. Not me and not the people downstairs. Doesn't she know about that, or she's just too greedy, stupid and just flipping doesn't care. What a bitch."

Roberto sighed, "Well at least I have an alien registration number now."

Ronald said, "Congrats friend, just continue to do what you're doing and I'll see if I can break the faucet in the bathroom."

They both laughed.

It was the letter that USCIS mentioned they will mail for Roberto as an answer to his application. He was required to submit an I-687. He submitted the application form as part of the process. After waiting a couple of months, he received a letter from USCIS stating that his application was denied, whatever fees he paid were not refundable. He was advised to file form I-694 for appeal. Again, he needed to pay a non-refundable fee of $890.

He thought of going to the southern border—he heard in the news that the people who crossed the border got processed over there. But he can't, he needed to go to work and send money to his Mom. After all the rigorous ordeal with USCIS, he finally decided to go to the lawyer this time.

CHAPTER TWENTY-FIVE

Pursuing Hope

He set up an appointment with Atty. Rezontory in Newark. He consulted that same lawyer ten years ago. He didn't get any help from that lawyer. This time he thought he can get some advice—he was filing form I-485.

Atty. Rezontory said, "Everything you have in here doesn't mean anything. You just wasted your money filing for an appeal. I cannot help you."

Roberto said, "Can I apply for I-485?"

The lawyer asked, "Based on what?"

Roberto said, "This petition, I am a derivative of this petition."

The lawyer asked, "Did your mother come in this country?"

Roberto answered, "No."

The lawyer asked, "Do you have any friends who can file a petition for you, a house or a company that can sponsor you?"

Roberto said, "They didn't want their financial documents submitted to immigration. They don't want to do anything with my status."

The lawyer asked again, "Do you have a girl-friend or a boyfriend?"

Roberto said, "No."

The lawyer said, "I really cannot do anything for you. But don't lose the petition papers, it may help you eventually."

It was a consultation that lasted twenty minutes and costed $130. He knew he won't get anything, but he tried anyway. He went home and reviewed the application form, he pursued to file the I-485 anyway.

He didn't say anything to anybody at work that he had filed all these shit with USCIS. Ronald knew, but as a good friend to Roberto—he kept quiet about it. Roberto received updates online regarding his application.

He texted Landlady Josephine, "USCIS updated me about my application. The online notice said that I will receive a notice in the mail."

Landlady Josephine replied, "Ok, I'll let Gemma know."

He was lucky—it was Ronald who checked the mail. Roberto found his packet inside his bedroom. He knew Ronald inserted the packet under his bedroom door. He received a notice that his application fee was not correct for I-485. Plus, he needed to specify the type of application he's submitting.

CHAPTER TWENTY-SIX

Persistent Pain

He called his Mom to let her know about the I-485. "Hey Mom."

Kevin was the one who picked up the phone, "Hello Roberto. It's Kevin."

Roberto asked, "How are you? How's Mom? Did you guys liked the stuff I sent? Did the kids finish eating the chocolates?"

Kevin said, "Mom can't talk right now. Rizza died of complications from her condition. Yes, we received the box already. Sorry we're not able to let you know sooner. When her foot got amputated, it wasn't too long until her leg was next. She didn't wait to really get better when her thigh got cut afterwards. She suffered a serious complication from her condition, until she can't make it anymore. Her lungs failed, got filled with water or something, I don't know. They couldn't do anything for her anymore. Dad is hurt, Mom is hurt—I don't know what to do. My own chest is hurting too, sometimes I can't breathe."

Roberto can't talk he only said, "I'll call again."

He wept bitterly, he remembered Virginia. But he cannot dwell on her memory. Rizza's death devastated him just the same. But just like the pain he felt due to Virginia's death he cannot function and yet he forced himself to get up and go to work.

Boss Gerry and Marlenny learned what happened to Roberto's sister. They were shocked, she was just a young soul. Rizza was older than Roberto but at 60 she was still young to die. They encouraged Roberto to stay focused. The unpredictability of life was just something that needed to be accepted by anyone, whatever the circumstances were—big or small, good or bad.

Boss Gerry wanted him to take a week off, but he refused. He can't stay at home and do nothing. He doesn't want to give Gemma anything to report to Landlady Josephine.

CHAPTER TWENTY-SEVEN

Still Hopeful

He was busy at work but managed to run his errands—post office, bank, laundry, grocery shopping and all that stuff. Gemma and the owners of the house had a lot of gossips going on. But Roberto managed to ignore all of what's going on around him. He knew the pain that he felt from the death of loved ones was very unforgiving. He thought this time he was strong enough.

Weeks passed by when he received the packet from USCIS. He didn't feel enthused about it anymore. He knew he needed to provide more information or he thought it was another denial. It was returned to him because USCIS was requiring him to submit a complete payment which he did not include the money order of $85 for the biometrics fee. He mailed it back and was again returned to him.

This time he knew what it was, USCIS won't process the application not until he specified the application type. He was right this time with his thoughts about the application type. He put it away, he doesn't know what to do. He didn't know the receipt number—there was no receipt number given to his Mom by Aunt Paula neither by the immigration office. He didn't know his Mom's alien registration number either. There wasn't one. To his frustration, he decided to take his time. He did not do anything to it, he just kept the motion of his life—work and then home activity.

He thought of filing a G-369, but even that—he took time in filling out the form. He sent an email to her niece.

Dear Chelsey,

Please print out the attached authorization letter that Mom needs to sign, have her sign it. I need it for the G-369 that I am submitting to obtain Mom's receipt number and alien registration number if she has any of these two. Maybe, just maybe—USCIS will finally be happy. I am praying to the LORD that I can get a green card through this petition.

Thanks very much,
Uncle Rob

Chelsey replied. She attached the signed authorization letter in her email. She also attached a photo of the letter from immigration addressed to her grandma. Her grandma had the immigration letter all along—it was kept in a plastic envelope for a long time. Roberto didn't know anything about it, when he downloaded the documents he saw the case number of the petition indicated at the bottom of the page. Roberto rejoiced, finally he has the case number of his Mom's petition clearly typed on a piece of paper. He decided not to do anything with any of it yet. He was just so tired of not knowing what to do to satisfy the requirements of USCIS.

He finished his day's work and decided to call home.

He called his Mom, "Hello."

Mom said, "Oh hi my son. How are you doing?"

He said, "I'm ok Mom. I can't forget Rizza and I remember Virginia."

Mom said, "Don't punish yourself my boy. I know how much it hurts but we cannot do anything about it—but accept it."

Roberto said, "I know Mom, but it hurts. I can't understand why we have to go through this. Do I need to go through this?"

His Mom said, "Our lives has its highs and lows. If we keep on having good times—is there anything that we can learn from those moments? If we keep on having difficulties—we get challenged, we stay up to fight or we accept defeat. It's like a box of chocolates you know, you don't know if you'll like what you have picked."

Roberto can only say, "Oh Mom."

Mom said, "What can we do? Do we succumb to pain? Or do we continue living? I'd choose to stay standing, and you should too."

Roberto said, "I know Mom, I filed my I-485. I am waiting for any result, any result. Mom how's Dad?

Mom said, "Don't lose hope, your Dad felt sad about what happened with RIzza. But he's still fighting. He's staying alive—just like John Travolta. But of course, he's not getting any better. But I know he's lucky because he's still alive. Your sister was just not able to cope up anymore. It was sad and my heart is aching but—what can I do. I cannot turn back time. Her little buy-and-sell store still runs, Kevin is operating it. At least we have a little bit of income. Thank you always for your support, especially the box. We love all the stuff."

He still didn't forget that he had to do something about the USCIS packet.

He couldn't convince himself to act on it sooner. He just thought it might just be the same result—rejection. So why bother to submit it right away.

After a couple of weeks of frustration—Roberto just mailed the I-845 packet back by providing his Mom's date of birth, the date of the petition when it was filed, and the case number which was written on the front part of the petition document he submitted from the beginning. He mailed it, without any expectation of anything good will come out of it despite the hefty fee.

CHAPTER TWENTY-EIGHT

Connecting Ties

He searched Facebook if he can find Aunt Paula. He doesn't know her, neither her friends. He searched for Aunt Paula's husband—Uncle Cris. His Mom said that Uncle Cris's whole family was all over California. Uncle Cris divorced Aunt Paula and then remarried. They didn't have kids together. Where did Aunt Paula live in California and where was Uncle Cris and his siblings? Even if he was able to find them, what is he going to do? Would he go to California? How would he get there? He can't possibly take a week off without pay—more so he can't take two weeks off. But he kept searching, until one day he found Uncle Cris's sister's name in Facebook.

He called his Mom, "Hello Mom."

Kristina picked up the phone, "Hello."

Roberto said, "Kris it's me. Call Mom, where is she, I need to ask her something."

Kristina said, "Ok." Then she hollered at her Mom.

Mom said, "What is it?"

Kristina said, "Roberto wants to talk to you."

Mom took the phone from Kristina, "Hello my son, how are you?"

Roberto said, "Mom I found a name in Facebook, her name is Antoinette Rand. That's Uncle Cris's last name, right? And his sister was name Antoinette, is that correct?"

Mom said, "Yes, I think it's Toni. Yes, it might be Toni. You can try Roberto, try and see if they know where my sister is?"

Roberto said, "Ok Mom, how are you? How's Dad?"

Mom cried, "Your Dad had a mild stroke, with his condition those mild strokes are fatal. He cannot afford to have any more of those. If it happens again I don't know what I will do."

Roberto said, "Mom stop crying please. You are making me sad. I don't know where else can I look for hope, if I can buy some of it—I'll buy a truck load. Dad will not get better—but we can hope that he will still be around for long. I want to see him again, Mom. Don't lose hope."

Roberto sent a message to Aunt Toni through Facebook. He waited but there was no reply. He tried the online white pages, he found the same name with an address. He thought, he'd write her a letter. After a week of mailing the letter it was sent back to him.

Gemma said, "You have a returned letter from Toni Rand, she's your pen-pal in California?"

Robert said, "Thanks Gemma."

Gemma said, "Don't forget to invite us on your wedding."

Roberto said, "Of course."

He went in his bedroom. He was thinking—he got tired of thinking. He wanted to eat something. No, he didn't want to eat he just don't know what to think and what to do.

Roberto called his Mom again, "Mom, hello."

His Mom said, "Hello Roberto."

Roberto said, "Mom I will make a Facebook account under your name ok? Aunt Toni is not responding to my friend request. She returned my letter to me. I sent her a letter, she sent it back to me, maybe because she didn't know my name or she doesn't remember."

His Mom said, "Do whatever you need to do."

Roberto asked, "How are you doing? Dad's still the same? How's Kevin, he's been telling me that his chest hurt sometimes. Is that a heart condition too or he just hurt because he's crying?"

His Mom said, "We all go through serious stress here at home. Maybe it was too much stress he's experiencing. You know how it is over here. The weather is hot mostly and with everything that happened—your Dad's situation and your sister gone. He must have stressed out too much."

Roberto tried to send a friend request again to reach out to Aunt Toni using his Mom's name. A couple of days passed, Aunt Toni accepted Roberto's request. He sent a message in his Mom's behalf informing Aunt Toni to accept Roberto David's message if she ever gets one.

Roberto tried to send the letter back to Aunt Toni one more time. He had a new piece of envelope—he wrote down Aunt Toni's name and address at the center part of the back of the envelope. This time, he put his Mom's name and his name, on the top left corner of the envelope. He placed the same letter inside the envelope—the same letter that was sent back to him from the first attempt that he did.

Dear Aunt Toni,

My name is Roberto David. I am Aunt Paula Rand's nephew. If you remember Lily David—she's Aunt Paula's only sister, her only sibling. Lily David is my Mom. I live here in New Jersey. I don't have any family here except Aunt Paula who's in California. I was wondering if you can give Aunt Paula's address to me. I'd like to let her know that my Mom is ok. I'd like to know how she's doing as well. If you can connect with me on Facebook, I'd like to know how you're doing too.

Best Regards,

Roberto

He waited for a couple of days, the letter was not sent back to him this time. He was convinced that it was Aunt Toni's address and it was Aunt Toni—Uncle Cris's sister. He finally got a chance to connect to Aunt Paula this time around. Maybe Aunt Paula can help with some information in the petition.

Roberto had a message on Facebook. It was Aunt Toni.

She wrote, "Hi Roberto, it was so nice to know that you're here in the US. Although we're too far apart, I am happy to have known you were here. How are you? How's life in the east coast? Do you like it there? I hope you're not having a hard time at work. But don' you work too hard. When you get a chance send me a message. I'd like it if you connect with me on FB, I usually don't pick up calls when I don't know the number. But here's my cell number—331-555-1234. You can send me a text message so I can add you to my contact list."

He replied back, "Hi Aunt Toni. I am so glad that I finally received a message from you. I have been trying to look for Aunt Paula for the longest time. My Mom didn't know what happened to her. They lost contact, I searched for her in Facebook but I can't find her. I am so glad I found you. Aunt Toni, I hope you don't mind me asking you a favor. I was wondering if Aunt Paula can still remember her petition for my Mom. Only if you get a chance to talk to her, may I please ask you a favor to ask Aunt Paula about it."

Roberto didn't wait for a reply from Aunt Toni. But he knew that she would reply again. He thought of calling his Mom to tell her the good news.

Roberto rang his Mom's landline, "Hello."

Kevin answered the phone, "Hello."

Roberto said, "Kev it's me."

Kevin said, "Roberto?"

Roberto said, "It's me. What's going on? How are you guys? Where's Mom? What's the noise that I'm hearing in the background?"

Kevin said, "Roberto, Dad is in the hospital. He can't breathe anymore. He said his chest was getting tight, he couldn't breathe. Maybel went to the hospital with Mom."

Roberto said, "Oh my god Kevin. I called because I am going to tell Mom the good news."

Kevin was crying and asked, "What is it?"

Roberto said, "I finally got a message from Aunt Toni in Facebook. I sent her a reply message but I'm not expecting her to reply back right away. I have a chance now to get in touch with Aunt Paula, finally the LORD heard my prayers. I am hoping that I might have a chance from this immigration process—if there's any chance at all. If not, at least I found Aunt Toni and Aunt Paula. And now I can't celebrate because of Dad's situation."

Kevin can hear Roberto's sniffles, "Roberto, stop crying. You can't lose hope. You've got to look at the light at the end of the tunnel. Whatever happens to Dad—put in your mind that it's part of the process. Please stop crying."

Roberto can't talk, he was sobbing. Kevin just hung up the phone, he didn't know what to do to pacify his brother. Kevin knew that Roberto wanted to see his Dad again—alive. No matter what the conditions were, Roberto dreamt of seeing his Dad and talk to him again and maybe laugh with him again.

CHAPTER TWENTY-NINE

Ruthless

Roberto wanted to share with his Dad the experiences he went through. How tough it was to live in a foreign land. What it's like to have fallen in love, how he coped up with vicious trials especially Virginia's death. He'd like to ask his Dad how did he stayed in love with his Mom all those years. He wanted to tell his Dad that he wanted the same thing, that was part of his dream. Roberto dreamt mostly, maybe he can bring all of his family in the US and stay there for the rest of their lives.

He can only cry, his dream once more was threatened by death. How would he be able to fight death? His Dad's youth passed by already, so did his Mom's. He doesn't want to think that death was the only thing waiting for them both because of their age. But no, they can still dream, not his Dad. He thought it might be his Dad's last couple of days, he doesn't know. He did not want to think about it, but it's evident. He still doesn't want to think about it—but it kept crossing his mind. He didn't know if he would call his Mom again, or talk to Kevin again or to any of them. But he needed to let her Mom know that he would stand. In the midst of the storm—he will stay standing.

He tried to calm himself down. He'd still work without telling anyone. He called his Mom after a few days, maybe his Dad would make it, if he's still alive he would be in a vegetative state at least he's still alive.

Roberto said, "Hello Mom."

Maybel his oldest sister answered, "Hello."

Roberto said, "Mom it's me."

Maybel cried and said, "Roberto its Maybel, Dad is gone. He died yesterday. His body was not responding to any medications, his heart weakened—they tried to resuscitate but there was no heart beat anymore. I'm sorry Roberto—you don't deserve this news, but Dad's gone. I know how painful this is for you, but you've got to stay strong. Mom can't talk right now. I will tell her that you called, I'll let her know that maybe when the phone rings again it might be you. Maybe by that time she's ready to talk. I was wondering if you can tell Aunt Toni about what happened—only if you're ready to talk about it. I'm sorry Roberto. Kevin is with Mom, he's trying to control his chest pain. He doesn't know why he's having chest pains. Maybe because of pressure and the situations that's been happening."

Roberto said, "Please tell Mom I called. If she's not ready to talk right now, I'll call again. Do you guys need anything? I'll send money again, but besides money what else can I send to all of you? I can send it through LBC. Who's with Dad?"

Maybel said, "Aunt Regina's with Dad. She helped us paid some of the bills, but not fully paid yet. She's Dad's only sister who helped, the others can't—you know how it is. Try to call tomorrow."

Roberto said, "Ok."

Roberto's heart was broken into million pieces. His grief was unbearable but he needed to be up and about. He went to work as usual. He tried to be the same, but everybody can feel something through his quietness.

Marlenny asked, "Roberto are you ok? You're pretty quiet, you looked like you're so deep in your thoughts. Talk to me."

Roberto said, "I don't know girl. I don't know if I'm confused, or am I angry or mad or just tired."

Marlenny asked, "Why? What's the matter? What made you tired? I can help you with your tasks. For today you won't sweep the dining I'll do it for you. I'll let Jayson answer the phone while I sweep the dining. Will that help you?"

Roberto said, "That's ok girl, I got it."

Marlenny said, "No, I'll do it—I don't take your no answer as an answer. You understand what I'm saying? Now what's the matter."

Roberto couldn't hold it anymore, "I can't bear the thought that my sister died and I won't see her again and now my Dad died.

Marlenny exclaimed, "What? When? What happened? How come we don't know anything about this. How come you're not saying anything. Aren't we included in your life? We are your friends, no not friends, your family here."

Roberto was crying and said, "I don't know. I thought all along that there's a solution for every problem. I thought I can wait for the solutions to come along."

Marlenny said, "Oh my god, Roberto. I am so sorry. We didn't know, why we didn't know—I don't know. Why are you hiding yourself from us?

You're grieving and we don't know anything about it. You know we will help you."

Roberto said, "I know you will help me. But it's been too much help that you guys have been giving me. I don't know how to ask for more. I don't know why this is happening and all I can do is ask help from all of you. I got tired of bad things happening to me, I thought I'd take a rest in asking for more favors. But it just keeps coming, no room to breath—then here comes another jab."

Marlenny said, "No Roberto, we all help each other here. If what's happening to you happened to me, are you going to stop helping me, of course not. Lucas had been asking for help non-stop, the kind of situation you're in—we're here for all of you, for all of us."

Roberto said, "I don't know anything anymore— oh my god I am so tired"

Marlenny said, "I know you are. I know you have been pushing yourself to support your family. But I didn't know that their conditions were beyond bad. I didn't know if they were sick, very ill or what? Now I know."

Roberto said, "I'm sorry."

Marlenny said, "Oh honey don't say sorry to me. I should be the one who should say sorry to you. You are one mean fighting machine. You are here—this is not your home, you're trying to make it, you're a hard worker and then your family members started going. If that happened to me, I have lost it a long time ago, believe me, I'm gone beyond Pluto. I would have picked up all those drinking glasses and slammed all of them on the floor. Then you will have a lot of sweeping to do."

Roberto chuckled and said, "I will let you know what's going on next time."

Marlenny said, "No, there's no more next time like this. Just tell me whenever you think you have a situation that makes your heart heavy. I will do something to help you if I can—I can also make you laugh a little bit."

Roberto said, "Thank you, I know I can depend on all of you."

Marlenny said, "Of course you can. I will talk to the boss later ok."

Marlenny hugged Roberto, she shook his hair on his head with the palm of her right hand. She thought of herself as a big sister to everybody in the pizza store, she knew she's got to look after those kids, well most of the workers at the pizza store were younger than her and the boss. Roberto finished his shift, he went straight home. He was hoping that his Mom would be ready to talk this time. He was about to open the front door, when Gemma walked out of the house.

Gemma said, "Hi Roberto, no invitations from Toni Rand yet? Don't forget we are waiting for the invite. Plus, it would be good for you, you can get a green card when you get married to a US citizen."

Roberto knew he needed to keep his calm, "Ok." he said.

SIDE COMMENT: He can't possibly pick up a rock and throw it at Gemma's forehead. He knew he's not David—he wasn't fighting Goliath. He's fighting a dwarf— not so much effort is required.

He went inside the house before Gemma can open her mouth again. He checked the time, he waited a little bit. He was thinking of settling first, put his backpack beside the bed. He took off his uniforms and changed into house clothes. He gauged himself if he wanted to eat something first before calling his Mom. He took a slice of white bread from the fridge and toasted it. He thought that would keep him for an hour or two. He dialed his Mom's number.

He said, "Hello."

Kevin picked up the phone, "This is Kevin, who is this?"

Roberto said, "Kev it's me. How's Mom doing?"

Kevin said, "Mom is in the funeral home with Maybel and the kids. Dad will stay there one more day. Then he will be finally laid to rest."

Roberto said, "I called because I thought Mom would be home. Is she ok now, I mean she's ready to talk?"

Kevin said, "Yes, she's been talking to guests. Her friends from church and our neighbors encouraged her. Maybel and I talked to her too, we need to work together in this. We're so glad she listened."

Roberto said, "I'm glad too. At least we have one bit of good news for a change."

Kevin asked, "Did you talk to Aunt Toni yet? Are you ready to talk to others about what happened?"

Roberto said, "I forgot about Aunt Toni, I thought I'd give my grief a little time until I cope up then I'd tell the whole world about it. I told my coworkers. The front counter help was persistent, she bombarded me with questions. I thought if I didn't tell her what happened she will ask her husband to sit down with me, he's a cop. I find it funny, I thought I shouldn't be laughing but I thought at the same time I need to laugh. Otherwise, I'd lose my sanity."

CHAPTER THIRTY

Just a Quiet Soul

Roberto's Mom was suffering from the compounded grief that her family went through. Although she's cordial to everybody, she can't stop thinking about how painful it was not just for her but her children too. It doesn't matter if they're already grown, they haven't had time to grieve her daughter's death, now the father of her children.

Roberto was having his break time, eating a slice of plain pizza. He sat at the table close to the glass window of the pizza store. Julieta came in the front door. She walked to where Roberto was sitting.

She said, "Roberto hi, how are you holding up? I heard what happened and I am so sorry. I apologize for not having time to talk with you lately, I have been busy. I hope you don't mind me sitting down. You have been with me and Olivia for quite some time now. I want you to know that we're here for you. If you need support we're ready to support you, I know you know that. I don't want to say this—but don't get upset when I say, that you don't have to carry all these burdens by yourself. That's why you have friends, that's why you have us, that's why we're here. We're basically your family here. How easy it would be if we help each other out. I'd like for you to know something and this is between the two of us, Gerry is upset that you're hurting. If he could have done something he would have done it. You know how he supports his staff, right? But I told him that your privacy must be respected, not that you don't care or we don't care. But that matter is yours. However, we really felt bad because we couldn't do anything because we didn't know. I just hope we can help you in every way we can with whatever you need, ok. You know how I thank God that Marlenny is like that, sometimes nosy but good hearted. She didn't mean anything bad but she won't stop asking not until she gets the answers. I can't blame her—her husband is a cop."

Roberto chuckled, "I'm sorry too. I never knew that this is going to happen so soon. I mean it was bound to happen but not like this, I'd like to grieve for my sister a little bit but when my Dad followed my mind was cramming in overcoming the hurt, the pain, the sadness, the thought that they won't come back anymore and all other stuff. All I have were memories. I thought I could at least see my sister once more and hug my Dad again. But immigration is tough."

Julieta asked, "What have you done so far? Have you applied for your green card yet?"

Boss Gerry was at the front counter said, "Hey you two, having a good talk?"

Julieta said, "Oh no, why did he have to get out of the office right now? Hi honey. Roberto, I have to go talk to Gerry. When you clean the house next week I'll try to be there early. Maybe I won't go to Olivia's so I can talk to you. I'll see you ok."

Roberto said, "Thanks very much Julieta."

CHAPTER THIRTY-ONE

Pressing On

He was debating if he'd let Aunt Toni know about what happened to his Dad. Maybe he should tell Aunt Toni and she can relay the message to Aunt Paula. He checked his Facebook as soon as he got home.

Aunt Toni's message, "How have you been? Sorry I haven't been sending messages that often. I was busy but I will try to send messages more often. I hope you're doing ok."

Roberto replied, "Hi Aunt Toni. I know you're busy and I understand. How are you?

Aunt Toni replied, "Oh good you're online. I am off today, I did most of my errands in the morning and at noon I usually take a nap and get on my gardening or yoga. I used to walk in the park with your

Aunt Paula. But she suffered from Alzheimer's—when it got worse I had her stay in a nursing home.

Roberto replied, "Oh no. Aunt Paula can't remember clearly anymore."

Aunt Toni, "Yes, that was the problem. She was living by herself in an apartment not too far from mine, that's why we walked together at the park. But when her condition got worse she's bound to stay in the nursing home. I can't take care of her, I have a part time job. I needed the additional income to support myself. I helped her get to the nursing home, you know how it is. She has enough to pay the nursing home's fees. Is there something that you need from your Aunt Paula?"

Roberto replied, "Actually yes. I'd like to ask her if she has the copies of the petition papers that she filed for my Mom. I needed the receipt number and my Mom's A-number if there's any or if she knew about it. But I guess she won't know now."

Aunt Toni said, "Oh no. I don't think she had anything of that sort in her stuff at the nursing home. I don't know, I'm not sure. If I can find something I'll let you know. How's your Mom?"

Roberto replied, "Thanks Aunt Toni—I really hope the papers are still around. I needed them for my application. Mom was getting a little bit cordial as days pass by."

Aunt Toni asked, "What do you mean, she's been a nice person and she won't change."

Roberto said, "I really don't know how to tell you but I will. My sister Rizza died after which my Dad followed not too long ago. My whole family was devastated with what happened especially my Mom. My sisters and my brother said she has started talking to people again. We thought maybe she needed a little space to process things through."

Aunt Toni said, "I am very sorry Roberto, I am very, very sorry. I'm thinking you're on your own in the east coast and all these things are happening to you. Oh, I can imagine what you might be feeling right now. But stay strong, I will see what I can do here in this part of the globe."

Roberto said, "Thanks Aunt Toni."

Aunt Toni said, "I will try. Talk again later. Bye."

CHAPTER THIRTY-TWO

New Course

Roberto heard a knock on his bedroom door.

Ronald said, "Hey man, Sheila is here is that alright with you?"

Roberto said, "The owners know?"

Ronald said, "No, I asked her to dress and act like a boy."

They both laughed. Roberto said, "No problem man."

Roberto hollered, "Yo."

Sheila went out of the bedroom and said, "Hi."

Ronald said, "Roberto this is Sheila my steady girlfriend."

Roberto said, "My lips are sealed."

They all laughed. Sheila was a simple girl, she doesn't wear make up because it takes so much of her time—according to her. She wears her wavy blond locks from her crown down to her shoulders. She's not slim but not too heavy either.

SIDE COMMENT: What the heck—not slim but not too heavy—is this body shaming or what? No it's not body shaming—it's just a description. The readers have to know how Sheila looks like.

Ronald thought of finding Roberto a girlfriend—he can marry for real or just for green card.

Sheila asked, "Roberto doesn't have a girlfriend?"

Ronald said, "He had one. I don't know what happened."

Sheila said, "My friend—can we make them meet?"

Ronald said, "I'd like for you to find him a girl who will at least give him a fiancé visa. Don't just look for a girl that will be his girlfriend then reject him because of he's out of status. I personally don't want that for him. He will go through the whole caboodle of dating then the girl will find out he doesn't have a green card—then break with him. No. If you know a girl whom you want to introduce to him, let that girl know right away that he's out of status. If she wants to pursue the friendship then much better otherwise don't even bother. You can feel it when a girl is kind or not—you're good at that—I'm not."

Sheila said, "What do you mean you're not?"

Ronald chuckled. They were a good pair. They were both kind to Roberto and concerned too. They both hoped they can help Roberto but cautious not to overstep the boundaries.

Olivia went to the pizza store. She was sorry for Roberto's loss, she gave him money to alleviate his financial burden even if it was just a little amount. Just like the old saying goes, 'every penny counts'. Roberto really felt loved by the people around him. Olivia was thinking about filing a petition for Roberto, she'd like to try to post as her employer being a permanent help in her house—a yard worker and housekeeper. She was willing to help Roberto but she was weighing down the expenses that she can incur by doing so. Nevertheless, she tried.

She told Roberto about it. She filed ETA Form 9089, there was a news-paper that was delivered to her door step by mistake—she perused through the advertisement and found the landscaping vacant position to be filled. Fred and Olivia submitted the paper works to a lawyer, then they needed to wait.

The processing time was a killer, it will take months before they can receive the approval or denial.

Roberto now became more inspired. He'd like to tell Aunt Toni and his Mom and the whole world about the help that he got from Olivia. He continued his service to the pizza store and to his house cleaning bosses.

CHAPTER THIRTY-THREE

Decision Making

He received a message from Aunt Toni. She wrote, "Roberto how are you doing? I'd like for you to know that your Aunt Paula fell, she broke her hip and is now at the hospital. She's been taken care of, but I don't know what will happen yet. If she gets better, will she need a hip replacement? I actually don't know what decision to make because I am not her direct family, I don't know if your Mom can make decisions for her. But your Mom is too far away to be asked about decisions to be made. I'll let you know about any updates regarding Aunt Paula. In the meantime, take care of yourself. Don't get sick, don't work too hard. Always take it easy. It's difficult when you get sick, you know?"

Roberto replied, "Hi Aunt Toni thank you for the update on Aunt Paula's situation. I know it wasn't good news at all. But I appreciate you telling me. I have received help from one of my bosses. She helped me file for a green card or something. She said that it's better to try than not to try at all. I thought of telling you about it, I'll talk to my Mom later about it. Thanks again.

He called his Mom, "Mom, hello. Mom"

Kristina answered, "Hello."

Roberto said, "Is Mom around, it's me Roberto."

Kristina hollered, "Mom, it's Roberto. He's on the phone, Mom."

Roberto said, "How's everybody doing?"

Kristina said, "My kids are rowdy, the oldest one is already a teenager but thinks like he's a toddler. Can't stop playing with his baby brother."

Roberto said, "Oh Kristina it's you. I thought its Maybel. I have to tell Mom about Aunt Toni's message."

Kristina said, "Here's Mom."

His Mom said, "Roberto how are you, my son?"

Roberto said, "I've received help from my house cleaning boss. She started the filing of papers for sponsorship. She said maybe I can get a boost by what she did. Since I am still waiting for the result of my I-485, she might as well try. She said she will let me know when we will split the expenses for the filing and lawyers' fee. Mom Aunt Paula broke her hip. She fell and she's in the hospital. Aunt Toni doesn't know what decision to make if Aunt Paula gets better—can she still have hip replacement?"

Mom said, "No, she's already old to go through hip replacement. If she ended up sitting on a wheelchair and can't stand on her own, let her be like that. I am 88, she's 86. She's not gonna dance with John Travolta anymore, is she still going to twerk, no. She doesn't need a hip replacement. she will die in the process. Please tell Aunt Toni, to let her sit on a wheelchair when she gets better. We cannot do anything about it anymore. We cannot ask her about the petition she filed for me. We cannot bother her anymore. If she fights for her life then good. If she doesn't let her be. She's lived a full life already I suppose. It's time for her to take it easy. Let the nursing home take care of her. I can't be there for her, Toni needs to continue living, what else can we do?"

Roberto said, "Ok, Mom. I'll tell Aunt Toni what you said."

CHAPTER THIRTY-FOUR

Another Avenue

Ronald and Sheila found a girl who might want to help Roberto. They were scheming. Maybe they can throw a birthday party for Ronald in the house and invite maybe six of their friends to celebrate. But they have to know Roberto's schedule. They also thought of inviting Roberto out to dinner and celebrate, but Roberto was a busy bee. They tried to plan different shindigs so Valerie can meet with Roberto.

Ronald said, "Why don't we just eat at his work?"

Sheila said, "No, he will be distracted."

Ronald said, "I know, plus his schedule is so tight."

Sheila said, "Why don't we just do it at home?"

Ronald asked, "Which home?"

Sheila said, "Yours, of course."

Ronald said, "The rooming house? We will get in trouble. The people downstairs will call the cops due to rowdy crowd and noise complaint."

Sheila said, "We won't be noisy."

Ronald said, "Yeah, the two of us won't be noisy. Roberto won't be noisy. How about the other three? If Valerie won't be noisy then there's four of us. How about the other two? It's a party it's supposed to be fun. Noise and carelessness are part of it. But not in our rooming house."

Sheila said, "Then we just have Valerie come with us in the rooming house. We'll just have dessert—ice cream and cake maybe?"

Ronald said, "We can only try."

Roberto did all his connecting with his family and Aunt Toni when he's home. He'd like to check his phone once in a while, but he used his computer mostly to call his family. He didn't want other people to hear what he's saying, he doesn't want anybody to see if his sending messages to Aunt Toni. He was tired from work, he heard a knock on the door.

Ronald said, "Hey man, what's up?"

Roberto asked, "Is the faucet in the bathroom broke?"

Ronald said, "No, why?"

Roberto said, "Just checking. What's up with you?"

Ronald said, "We're gonna celebrate my birthday here at home, Sheila and I. I hope you can join us. Sheila's friend might come here, Valerie."

Roberto said, "I'll try. You know how it is with my two jobs. When is it gonna be?"

Ronald said, "Tomorrow."

Roberto said, "Tomorrow is your birthday. Darn I forgot, happy birthday man. Maybe I can ask my boss to put me on a half day tomorrow. I can't call out, they'd investigate thoroughly if I'd call out because they know I don't and I won't. I need the money man."

Ronald asked, "When is your day off?"

Roberto said, "I don't have a day off. I have two houses to clean on my one day off. The other home-owner is my sponsor so I can't disappoint her. I realized now that because she started to file paper works for me—I can't disappoint her."

Ronald said, "How come you didn't tell me?"

Roberto said, "Tell you what?"

Ronald said, "That you have a sponsor."

Roberto said, "Because it's just a labor certification. It's a long process, it will take years. Before you know it I'm dead by the time I get the approval. You know how it goes."

Ronald said, "But at least your boss backed you up, let's pray to GOD for a positive result. Now we can hold a double celebration."

Roberto said, "I can count on you that what we spoke about right now stays here and not going out."

Ronald said, "You can count on me, but we have to celebrate."

Roberto said, "Yeah, but not tomorrow."

Ronald asked, "Can you not open up an afternoon or an evening so we can celebrate?"

Roberto said. "I'll text my boss, then I'll text you."

Ronald was happy to learn about some development in Roberto's life. At least now he has a little bit of hope to look forward to regarding his status. He wanted to tell Sheila but he can't. He didn't tell Sheila about the labor certification. Ronald can only hope for the best.

Roberto went inside his bedroom, he turned on his computer and sent a message to Aunt Toni, "Hi Aunt Toni. How are you? My Mom said that it's not necessary for Aunt Paula to have hip replacement. She might not make it if she goes through under the knife at her age, that's what Mom said. I'd like to tell you that my room-mate is asking me to celebrate his birthday. There will be four of us, him and his girlfriend plus me and their other friend Valerie. I don't know if I can go because I haven't had a day off since I found my house cleaning job. I can only wait for the result of the paper works. How I wish I can get the result tomorrow, I wish that it's an approved result. How's Aunt Paula doing? I hope she gets better so I can see her. How I wish I can travel, if only I can afford it."

Roberto was surprised when he saw Aunt Toni wrote a reply, "Hi Roberto. I am happy that you have a prospective change in your life. You can find a good friend in Valerie if that's what they're trying to do. You've got to give it a chance. Life is too short, we can't take it for granted. Your Aunt Paula got weaker and weaker. She stayed in the hospital so medical staff can monitor her progress. I don't want to be the bearer of bad news. But sadly, your Aunt Paula passed away 36 hours ago. Her heart fainted, they can't resuscitate—she had a DNR signed even before she had the serious ordeal with Alzheimer's. Please don't feel bad, I think this is what your Mom was saying. She did not deserve to suffer anymore. Although everybody's life differs from one another—I believe she lived her full life. I might want to think that she still wanted to live, but our lives can only last as far as GOD has numbered our days. Don't be discouraged about what happened, the pain will go away someday. But even if the wound is still fresh, don't let your heart bleed to defeat. Live, continue living. Always look forward to a new day. You never know, one day you'll receive an approval from immigration or department of labor or you might find a new best friend. Please tell your Mom how sorry I am. I can imagine the thought of them two never saw each other again. Don't look at Aunt Paula as the only source of your approved petition, changes always happen. You never know the change that our government will do in the future. Maybe by that time—it will bring some benefit to you. Don't lose hope. If you want, I can contact my daughter Melissa in Texas. We have not spoken in a long time, the reason why, I'll tell you about it next time. I will let you know if she will respond to my calls or texts. Stay strong, GOD is always on our side."

Roberto can't respond to what he just read. So many thoughts running through his head. It was another sad news but he knew he needed to go on with his life. He opened his bedroom door, he sat on the chair facing the dining table. He rested his elbows on top of the table, with his fingers interlaced and his hands clenched together, he closed his eyes and touched his forehead with his phalanx from crossed thumbs. It was not easy but he still had a future to look forward to, just like what Aunt Toni said.

He was thinking about going to Texas, maybe it's better there. But it would mean for him to start all over again. He never met Melissa. He doesn't even know that Aunt Toni had a daughter. Maybe Melissa, can help him find a girl to get married with.

He wanted to call his Mom. He doesn't know who to talk to. He thought of calling the sisters, but he won't, he doesn't want to bother them with his personal shit. He thought of dealing with it on his own first. Then he will tell the whole world again later. How would he take this trial? It seems like the more he wanted to see the members of his family the more he's losing them—one by one. Should he stop thinking about them? Should he stop caring? Must he think that this kind of situation is normal. Should he start getting numb, feeling numb? He doesn't have any answers. He's just going back to work—which was what he always did.

CHAPTER THIRTY-FIVE

Very Sad News

Two days passed he convinced himself that he needed to tell his Mom, it's now or never. He managed to collect himself and connected with his family.

Roberto said, "Hello."

Maybel said, "Hello, who is this?"

Roberto said, "It's me Roberto. Where is Mom?"

Maybel cried, "Mom and Kristina are in the hospital. Kevin was suffering from severe chest pain he cannot breathe. Mom thought it would be best to bring him to the hospital. He went through extensive tests. The doctor determined the cause. He has multiple blocked arteries, that's what Kristina told me when she called to give me some update. The doctors don't want to do angioplasty, they told Mom that Kevin needs an open-heart surgery. Kevin can get a massive heart attack that can leave him incapacitated or kill him. His angiogram procedure was expensive Rob. Mom paid for everything. Aunt Regina can't help for now. She said when she has recovered with her credit card bills—she'd help."

Roberto said, "Stop crying Maybel. I will try to send more help."

Kristina said, "You've been sending us help more than you can imagine. It's just that, I don't understand what's going on. It feels so heavy we can't take it anymore."

Roberto said, "We will get by, Aunt Toni said—don't lose hope."

Kristina asked, "How's Aunt Toni? Did she say anything about Aunt Paula?"

Roberto said, "Aunt Paula just died four days ago. I was debating if I need to tell Mom or not. But of course, she has to know. But not in this situation, but if not now, when? She has to know sooner or later, right? I don't know what to do Maybel. Sometimes I just want to feel nothing even if hurts so much I just want to ignore everything and think all this is normal. Everybody hurts in different ways. Nobody is left untouched."

Kristina sobbed, "Oh my god Roberto. Why is this happening? I don't understand."

Roberto said, "Stop crying, there's nothing we can do—just like what Mom said."

Kristina calmed down a bit and asked, "When do we tell Mom?"

Roberto said, "I don't know. Maybe when they get back from the hospital. Maybe Kevin will stabilize for a little while, when both Kevin and Mom had a day's rest then you can tell them. But not right away, Mom might get panicky."

Kristina said, "Ok. How are you doing?"

Roberto said, "I will be fine, don't worry about me.

CHAPTER THIRTY-SIX

Surprise

He was working continuously in the kitchen. Marlenny hollered for him to take his break. He forgot that break hours were part of his benefit even if he's out of status. He sat down on the table by the window without any food to eat. He was thinking about the calls that his lawyer he had been ignoring. He was trying to procrastinate in speaking with the lawyer thinking that it will just be another denial. His lawyer never left a message, but in his mind, it was always the lawyer's assistant who called anyways. He thought maybe the lawyer's office will eventually send a letter to Olivia or to him. Marlenny handed down a paper plate with a slice of cheese pizza on it.

Marlenny said, "I know something happened again. When you're ready to talk about it, we're here to listen. You better eat that shit and get your own iced tea ok."

Roberto smiled and said, "Thank you."

He went home—surprised about the three people in the rooming house. He forgot that it was the day of celebration. The date that he texted Ronald about his free evening. He said he would go home straight from work and would be ready to join them in the party. He was an hour late, he extended his time at the pizza store thinking that he doesn't have anything to do at home anyway. He won't call his Mom, he wanted to give his mind and heart a repose before connecting with her again. He wanted to sound comforting to his Mom by doing so. However, the desserts on the table surprised him.

Ronald and Sheila introduced Valerie, "Roberto you're late, this is Valerie."

Roberto said, "Hi guys, I'm sorry I completely forgot. There are extra work at the pizza store—I thought of having my hands on them to make sure that tomorrow they're not there waiting for me. Hi Valerie, how are you? How did you know these two?"

Valerie said, "Sheila and I used to work in the same building. She worked at the doctor's office and I worked at the restaurant downstairs."

Ronald walked in his bedroom, Sheila followed, they didn't close the door. They thought they'd rather hear what the conversation between Roberto and Valerie was about and they will give their two cents afterwards. Both Roberto and Valerie were cordial to each other. Even though Valerie doesn't work at the Café 24 anymore they both have something in common—restaurant. Valerie was holding a Supervisory position at a grocery store one mile away from the rooming house. Roberto seemed to enjoy the cake and ice cream, though Valerie didn't eat much. Time flew it's almost midnight, they all have to part ways. Sheila needed to drop Valerie off her house.

Ronald asked, "Do you want to stay here Sheila honey? We'll drop Valerie home then we'll come back here. It's too late for you to go home by yourself at this time."

Sheila said, "Let's drive Valerie home then we go to my place and sleep there. I'll wake you up early tomorrow so you can come back here to get ready for work."

Ronald said, "I'll get my work clothes and back-pack so that I can go to work tomorrow from your apartment."

Sheila said, "Better yet."

Roberto said, "Thanks guys, but I am so sorry for what happened. Nice meeting you Valerie."

Valerie said, "Nice meeting you too. Roberto, hope to see you again sometime."

Roberto said, "Ok."

Ronald said, "Come on people, let's go."

Ronald cleaned up. Before he went to bed, he sent a message to Aunt Toni. He hoped that Aunt Toni was ok.

Valerie was taller than Sheila. Her eyes were hazel brown. She had shorter hair—bob cut style. She doesn't wear full make-up, though she had a slight application of soft rose-gold eyeshadows on her eyelids. She's got a short black wing-liner at the corner of her eyes swept slightly upwards—resembling a Niké swoosh.

Boss Gerry was planning a catering event. Julieta's daughter was getting married. Her daughter was with her boyfriend for 15 years, they all thought it's about time.

Ronald and Sheila organized another shindig at the rooming house. Valerie was present, Roberto did not forget this time. He was more presentable this time. He wore one of the shirts he bought from Macy's Online—the reason why they got the twenty-five dollars monthly increase in rent. Ronald and Sheila did the same thing from before. They made sure that Roberto and Valerie are comfortable with each other—and then the two of them would slip away in the bedroom and leave the door open. Roberto and Valerie are enjoying their conversation, finally Roberto found another friend. He can't put his hopes high though.

CHAPTER THIRTY-SEVEN

Wedding Prep

Boss Gerry placed a printed-out sign on the front door. He posted it eight weeks ahead of time so that customers would know when not to call for orders.

TO OUR VALUED CUSTOMERS

WE WILL BE CLOSED ON APRIL 7
DUE TO A STAFF WEDDING EVENT
SORRY FOR THE INCONVENIENCE
WE'RE BACK IN BUSINESS—APRIL 8

Boss Gerry would be needing all the help that he can get to cater Dana's wedding. Roberto don't know anything about serving, but he still had four weeks to learn a trick or two from the servers or from Marlenny. He cannot just be a wall flower in the reception hall. No dishwashing will take place in the reception venue. He thought it would be great if Ronald and Sheila were there, including Valerie.

He called his Mom, "Hello."

Mom said, "Is this Roberto?"

He said, "Yes Mom it's me. I called because I want you to know that my schedule is getting hectic. The pizza store needs to cover a catering event. The whole staff are getting cross training, it means—I will be busy."

Mom said, "Ok, just don't wear yourself out."

Roberto said, "I won't—I love you Mom."

Mom said, "I love you too, we all love you."

The schedule was getting unbearable but they have to put up with it as the days passed. The sisters postponed the house cleaning so Roberto can focus on the catering and server tutoring from Marlenny.

He didn't have time to think about how painful it was to lose his sister, Dad, and Aunt without him seeing them before they go. Although he didn't forget his brother, he put aside his thoughts on how to help him due to the schedule.

Ronald asked, "Hey man, have I been seeing you, home or not? All of a sudden you became invisible. What's going on?"

Roberto said, "We're busy in the store. Boss Gerry's supposed step daughter is getting married. We need to make sure that we're ready when the day comes. There was no audition for catering—Julieta and her daughter both agreed that they will hire us for the event. My boss is really busy besides the regular operations we're having every day. It's very tiring, but we all need this. This is a good promotion for the store. Other people will see what else we can do apart from the regular gig we offer at the store.

Ronald said, "I get it man, I was just wondering where were you and what have you been doing. I'll check the mails if you want to, if I can get my hands on them. I won't open them I promise. You know what I mean."

Roberto said, "Sure you can. Thanks man, you're the best."

CHAPTER THIRTY-EIGHT

Life's Fragility

The dreaded wedding day came. Everybody was excited and stressed at the same time. Roberto was thinking about how wonderful it would have been if he married Virginia. But he realized that, preparing for the event was kind of hectic. He wondered how it would be like if he's the groom? How it would be like for his bride? All these thoughts flooding his mind.

He talked to himself, "Roberto you need to focus. There will be time for your day dreaming. Everybody might notice you again like you're on cloud nine. There's a lot of things that need to be done. Focus. Be careful not to drop anything this time. Every single item in your hand is important. Focus."

He took a couple of deep breaths and hustled.

The delivery van-1 was parked in front of the store, all food items need to be stored in van-1. Delivery van-2 was across the street. All chafing dishes, silver wares, and non-food items need to be stored in van-2, as well as staff items. Everybody needed to be aware of their surrounding before crossing the street.

There was a bit of traffic. The 66 and 94 buses came on both opposite sides of the street. There were cargo trucks and regular vehicles passing on that four-stop intersection. A lot of times there were drivers who sped through a red light. This was one of those days.

Ronald went home and checked the mail. There was a letter from Roberto's lawyer.

Ronald called Roberto instead of texting him, "Hey man, you have a letter from your lawyer."

Due to Roberto's excitement—he asked, "Ronald open the mail. Read it to me."

Ronald hesitated, "I'll wait for you later man. You've got to be the one to open this. It's yours not mine. I want to see your excitement later. I can feel this is a very good news. I can feel it man. See you later, break a leg. Do your best as you always do."

Boss Gerry kept updating everybody. The bride and groom were on their way to the church. The guests were already in the church, the parents were with their respective kids. Olivia was with Julieta and Dana. There were guests that went straight to the reception venue. Olivia decided not to stay long in the church and drove herself to the reception hall. Boss Gerry wanted some finger foods to be delivered right away to the reception so the guests can nibble on something. He knew that the open bar started as soon as people arrived.

Ronald called Sheila, "Hey babe, Roberto got a letter from the lawyer."

Sheila asked, "How do you know?"

Ronald said, "He's been busy lately due to the wedding that his boss booked. They're the caterer."

Sheila said, "That's a good one. How did you know it's from the lawyer?"

Ronald said, "The envelope says so. I told Roberto I'll keep an eye on our mails—mine and his. Before other people take it and open it again without Roberto's consent."

Sheila said, "Makes sense."

Roberto was carrying the last four glass bottles of sparkling water. He embraced them all with his left arm pressing them to his chest. He had a couple of wine glasses on his right hand thinking that he would drink the sparkling water from a wine glass when they all get to the reception venue. He'd pretend he's drinking wine. He placed a stem in between his ring and middle fingers, the other one was in between his index finger and thumb then folded his right arm over his left.

Julieta ordered a dozen sparkling water for the staff to drink in-case they ran out. There was no space in van-1 for the bottles, it was fully packed not even four bottles could squeeze in. He needed to put these last items in van-2. As he crossed the street there was a pick-up truck that sped, it was a landscaping truck trying to beat the red light. Roberto took his steps carefully for he's carrying some delicate items. He got hit. Out of nowhere—the truck swoop Roberto off his feet from the ground. Both of his arms flung open, the bottles fell on the ground and broke. His right hand was still holding the wine glasses as if his brain told him to guard the wine glasses with his life.

Boss Gerry was standing behind van-1 to supervise what stuff went inside both vans when he saw Roberto being catapulted to the curb. Every bottle broke, the jagged edged glass pieces were all over the place. Roberto's right elbow bended towards his body. He fell to the ground face down landing on his right hand. The pressure of his body broke the wine glasses. The bowls broke, the sharp edges sunk into his torso. One wine glass was left with only the stem still connected to a broken base. It stabbed Roberto's chest and fatally pierced his heart.

Boss Gerry screamed with deep pain in his heart. His rage was both literal and emotional. He ran to where Roberto was, he wanted to touch him but can't move him. Boss Gerry reached for his cell phone and called 911. He was frantic, he was crying, he was babbling. Everybody was shocked. Marlenny called her husband, he was almost 1.5 miles from the scene. The Union Fire Department was almost 2 miles, when will help ever come?

Everybody stood still—stopped what they were doing, they actually don't know how to respond to what they were witnessing.

It was like forever taking place.

The Union Medical Emergency Unit was close by almost twelve strides away from the pizza store. Boss Gerry took Roberto's phone, Roberto was unconscious.

SIDE COMMENT: Wait a minute—twelve strides? What does this even mean? Is It like Usain Bolt strides? Because one Usain Bolt stride can be equal to twenty steps from me, you know—the writer of this story.

There was a loud siren from the fire trucks that passed by the church. Police cars were passing the reception venue and an ambulance turn the siren sounding so loudly—even the angels in heaven can hear it. They took Roberto, Marlenny requested her husband to go in the ambulance. Boss Gerry doesn't know what to do. Some staff were still in the kitchen. Although they heard the siren—they didn't seem to care. It was kinda normal to hear about accidents around that area. It was pretty normal for them— not knowing that this time they will be very affected with the accident. Marlenny took charge.

She said, "Boss—the show must go on. We will deal with the boy later. We cannot leave the bride high and dry. Pull yourself together, lead the rest of the staff. As soon as we get everything set—we will come up with a plan."

Boss Gerry with a crack in his voice said, "Good enough."

Marlenny hollered, "Jayson, go to the kitchen let Renz know what happened. Tell him to take Julian and Sydney to go with him in the venue—NOW. Tell him to hurry up because Chris is all by himself there, probably now he's panicking. He's been organizing shit, attending to the guests who arrived early and probably tipsy with the three little cans of White Claw he brought for himself."

Jayson ran to the kitchen—wishing he could turn back time. His mind was fazed about what happened to Roberto. They were good buddies. Roberto always covers for Jayson when he calls out. He looked at Jayson as his little brother. Roberto supported Jayson's artistry. He has nothing but plain admiration to that boy. Although at times—Roberto gets tired of Jayson's antics, he still can't say no to the young dude when he called-out.

CHAPTER THIRTY-NINE

The Show Must Go On

Boss Gerry's team finally made it to the venue. They were busy—not a minute wasted. They all have to focus because the show must go on. The guests are now arriving—one after the other. The merriment grew and each one greeted each other with smiles and warm hellos. The bride and groom's entourage finally arrived.

Julieta was looking for Roberto—she approached Boss Gerry, "Where is Roberto? Did he get left behind in the store? What else do we need here? He still needs to bring some more stuff?"

Boss Gerry was ignoring Julieta, "I am worried too." That was all he can say.

Julieta said, "He better be here—better late than never."

Boss Gerry asked, "Lucas where's Marlenny?

Lucas said, "I'll get her boss."

Marlenny approached Boss Gerry and said, "Boss, don't worry too much. I know the boy would want us to deliver our best today. We got this. You know Mike, he won't disappoint us. He will take care of Roberto—that's the kind of guy I married. Let's do this boss for the sake of the bride and Julieta."

Boss Gerry said, "I can't do it Len. I want to go to the hospital. Please take charge. I can't be beside Julieta and she keeps asking me, where is he? I can't tell Julieta what happened—I can't ruin this day. Just please take charge tell Julieta I went back to help the boy. Oh my god what's happening? His family and then him, oh my god. Of all people—why Roberto?"

Marlenny said, "Boss please stop that. I don't want anybody to see you like that especially Julieta, please."

Boss Gerry was restless, he kept pacing here and there, out of the kitchen going around the catering area, then pacing in the hallway and back to the kitchen. The guests were enjoying their time, Julieta and Olivia approached Boss Gerry.

Olivia said, "Gerry thank you for your help. The food is out of this world. Everybody's having fun and enjoying their meal. Thank you so much."

Boss Gerry said, "All the best for your family Olivia. This is Dana's special day. She deserved nothing but perfection."

Julieta said, "Why don't you join us?"

Boss Gerry said, "Olivia please excuse me, I need to talk to Jules."

Olivia nodded her head, Boss Gerry led Julieta ten steps away, "Jules I need to check on Roberto. I need to leave, please allow me to leave."

Julieta asked, "Where is he anyway?" Isn't he coming? Are there stuffs that need to be done in the store? Does he need to bring some extra stuff? It looks like everything is here."

Boss Gerry said, "That's what I'd like to know— if everything is ok with him. please I need to go."

Julieta said, "Why don't you just wait for him?'

Boss Gerry said, "I can't."

Julieta asked, "Why not?"

Boss Gerry said, "Julieta please just let me go. I wanted to go without telling you, but it might be a cause of another misunderstanding. I decided to let you know that I need to check on him so you would understand where I went."

Julieta said, "This is an important event, I want you to be here."

Boss Gerry said, "I know that, but it's important."

Julieta said, "What's important?"

Boss Gerry can't hold himself anymore—he cried and said, "Roberto was hit by a truck. I don't want to tell you because I want you to celebrate this day with your daughter and family and friends. I want to know if he made it or not or what is his condition. Please let me go, you know I love you. But I need to check on him too."

Julieta cried. She can only say, "Oh my god. Ok. Oh my god. Why Roberto? Why now? What happened? Oh my god, no. Not today, no."

She can't control herself. Boss Gerry embraced her tightly, he kissed her on her forehead. He tried to console her.

Boss Gerry, "Stop crying sweetheart. You'll ruin your make up. You've got to celebrate with Dana. Go and entertain the guests, I know they're expecting you to be around inside the hall. Go."

Julieta said, "Keep me posted. I love you"

Boss Gerry gently held her face with his both hands. He gazed in her eyes with a fierce look. He kissed her lips and said, "I love you very much."

CHAPTER FOURTY

Loving Hearts

He left her crying. He walked so fast to get out of the reception hall—nobody noticed him passing by. He was in the parking lot—he opened the door of his car, and sat inside. He was reaching for his phone at the back pocket of his pants.

He dialed Mike's number, "Hello Mike."

Mike answered and said, "Gerry."

Mike couldn't say anything, there was a long pause before he can even think of what he's going to tell Boss Gerry. He was thinking if he's still in the wedding reception he might holler at everybody. He doesn't know what to do until he heard Boss Gerry's voice on the phone again.

Boss Gerry said, "Mike, what's going on? What happened? Do you have any info? Is there any update? How's he doing?"

Mike can only stall for so long and said "He's gone Gerry. He's DOA. He's got concussions mostly on the upper part of his body. He dislocated a shoulder, cracked cheek bone, broken collar bone, cracked rib, and I don't know—it was brutal. The impact was sort of a heavy pounding like King Kong got his hand on a wrecking ball. These conditions though aren't serious—he could have survived. But his heart was pierced—he lost so much blood. I'm sorry Gerry, I really am. Marlenny's going to give me an earful later. She'll say I didn't give my everything. I'm a cop not the doctor, not even an EMT. If only I can do anything I would, I can only stand on the sideline you know. But I understand, this is very painful and incomprehensible. We've got a wedding and a run-away at the same time. I'm so sorry."

Boss Gerry cried. He threw his phone on the passenger seat. Mike can hear him on the other side. He held the steering wheel with both hands, he tilted his head backwards and screamed. He remembered his younger brother who died in the Gulf War. He should have convinced his brother not to go, at least he could have convinced his brother not to enlist.

But he can only stand on the sideline. His brother wanted to serve, wanted to protect the innocent in any way he can. Boss Gerry saw the same passion in Roberto's heart, his determination—his grit.

Ronald waited for Roberto to come home. Ronald can't wait to see what's the letter all about. He wondered why the lawyer would send him a letter, why can't Roberto be informed by phone call?

He called Sheila, "Honey, Roberto's not home yet."

Sheila said, "Just wait for him, don't get anxious. He will be home."

Ronald said, "I want to call him, just a quick chat and then I'll hang up."

Sheila said, "He might be busy at work. Why don't you just wait, you can ask all the questions you want when he's home ok."

The wedding merriment has gone to a conclusion. Boss Gerry went to Julieta's house. She opened the door and said, "Oh my god Gerry."

Boss Gerry stepped inside, they hugged each other and he asked, "Was everything perfect for Dana? Did you have a good time? How was everything, how was everybody?"

Julieta said, "It was perfect for Dana and everything was fabulous and fantastic. Except of course the accident. How was he? Is he getting any surgery or any bodily repair or something? Who was with him in the hospital? Can we see him tomorrow?"

Boss Gerry asked, "Can I sit down?"

Julieta said, "Of course, do you want something to drink?"

Boss Gerry said, "I'd like whisky."

Julieta said, "A strong drink?"

Boss Gerry said, "Please sweetheart, I'd like to drink tonight. I can stay overnight here, right?"

Julieta said, "Of course, mi casa es su casa."

Boss Gerry said, "Good, because I'd like to stay here for the rest of my life."

Julieta gave him the glass, "What's going on? Please tell me, I'd like to know what's in your mind. We can talk about anything and everything now that we've learned a lot from our past. Please Gerry, tell me."

Boss Gerry placed the glass on the coffee table and said, "Roberto's gone."

Julieta exclaimed, "What do you mean, gone?"

Boss Gerry placed his forehead on both palms, "Roberto died in the accident, Mike said he's DOA. I can't believe he's not coming back. He's a young man full of potential, at a young age—he couldn't even get a chance at his dream. All he did was to put himself last. It makes me think of Jimmy, before he was deployed for the fucking Dessert Storm. They were young men full of energy and life—only to die in their youth. They didn't even experience retirement. They could have known how it's like to retire. Oh my god."

Boss Gerry was sobbing, Julieta doesn't know how to calm him down. She was crying too. Crocodile tears were falling down her cheeks. She kept pacing back and forth from the kitchen to the living room, she was lost for a bit. She sat beside him, she put her right arm on his back smoothly massaging him. She placed her left hand on his left arm. She kissed his cheek, she pulled him closer to her. She tried to console him, she stood and took his left hand. He stood and followed her, she led him into her bedroom.

CHAPTER FOURTY-ONE

A Dear Friend

The following day, Ronald was knocking at Roberto's door. He kept knocking—there was no answer. He's pissed—he called Roberto's cell phone. He was beside Roberto's bedroom door thinking that he would hear the phone ring. Nobody picked up the call, he didn't even hear any sound from Roberto's bedroom. He was confused, he didn't know what to do.

He sent a text message for Roberto. "Hey dude, where are you? Did you get a chance to go home last night? Where are you? We need to talk. I have your letter."

Ronald received a broadcast text that wrote,

"To all of Roberto's friends, my name is Gerry. I own the pizza store where Roberto was working. I don't know how to tell you how deeply sorry I am for what happened. Roberto got hit by a truck yesterday that caused his passing.

He was a very hard-working man, he always puts himself last, that made him a true great friend. For me he's a brother and I am sorry to have lost another one."

Ronald doesn't know what to think, what to do. He called Sheila, "Honey, Roberto is dead."

Sheila said, "Ronald what did you just said? Are you going to work, are you at work now? Say that again."

Ronald was crying, "Sheila Roberto got hit by a truck, he died yesterday. Oh my god."

Sheila asked, "What? What happened? What? It's already June, you can't play April fools on me babe. Ronald, what are you talking about, oh my god, not Roberto! Ronald, please stop crying. No, not Roberto. Oh my god, I need to call Valerie. No, not today, maybe later." Sheila was panicking, she doesn't know if she was the one babbling or Ronald.

Ronald doesn't know how to express his sadness, he could only muster a bit of strength and said, "I opened the letter from the lawyer. It said that the labor certification was approved. He got the shot for his green card Sheila. He got the first step approved. He could have gotten it, he could have achieved his dream, oh my god. Why would a kind-hearted person die like that? Why would a good man be taken away from this world?"

Sheila asked, "How about his family? How will they know? Who will tell them?"

Ronald said, "I will ask Gerry who owns the number from the broadcast. I'll ask what happened, I can even go to the pizza store and ask. I will ask anybody Sheila. I will let you know. His Mom needs to know, oh my god. Why would this have to happen?"

Everybody in the store were grieving. Marlenny's heart was aching more so her head was aching so bad that her only two brain cells were gung-ho. Keeping themselves from collapsing to keep her sanity intact. This is the time that brain cell Bainy and brain cell Nainy thought they could rest. They were both chillin'—not sending strong electrical signals to each other. They were busy during the planning of the catering. Now that the wedding event was over the two of them can finally take it easy.

Bainy and Nainy were not able to reproduce. So, they just enjoyed each other's company from the time Marlenny was born during World War 2.

SIDE COMMENT: Will there be a story written about Nainy and Bainy?

The management want to close the store but they can't disappoint the customers. Their hearts and minds were confused about how to handle what happened. Was it supposed to be a happy feeling? Or not at all. Nobody wanted to tell Dana what happened, the whole world could only wish Dana the best.

Ronald got in touch with Roberto's Mom. He doesn't want to be the bearer of bad news but his family needed to know. Ronald doesn't know where to get the strength to talk to his family but he must get in touch with them especially with his Mom. Ronald was overwhelmed with sadness. His mind was playing tricks on him. Thoughts of getting a hammer and strike the bathroom faucet so hard until it breaks. He thought of how Roberto's life was so challenging and how Roberto could've made it.

He can't believe that his best friend will never come back.

Roberto's Mom wanted him cremated. They can't afford to pay for the shipping of his body. Boss Gerry said he will pay for everything, Roberto doesn't need to be cremated, but his Mom insisted. Ronald paid another month for Roberto's rent. He needed time to pack all of Roberto's stuff and send them all to his Mom.

It was very tragic for Roberto's family—but every grief is always followed by a new hope. Hope that we can hold on to as long as we can.

Thank goodness hope is free. Otherwise, I won't hold on to it for too long—because I know I'd be broke big time.

That's why I can only say, the unpredictability of life—is nothing but unpredictable.

By the way, are those side comments even allowed to be included in books?

The End

ACKNOWLEDGEMENTS

My dad—thank you for your love (may you rest in peace)

My mom—thank you for your care

My older sisters Marian and Miguelita—thank you for teaching me how to read an Eng-lish book at age 6 (may you both rest in peace)

My oldest brother, Miguel—thank you for your support (may you rest in peace)

My oldest sister, mercy—thank you for looking after me when I was little

My youngest brother, Leo—you should thank me for looking after you when you were little

Angeles Cepeda—thank you for nurturing me at a young age

Maryjane Cepeda—thank you for being my very best friend

Jayson Boone, Maranatha Jireh Domingo, Maria Helena Chin—thank god for your artis-tic talents, it challenged me

Charles Lowry, Linda Dale, Julian Rodriguez—thank you for your friendship

Tommy Demaio - thank you for giving me a chance to earn an honest living

Lu Vallejo, betty falcon, Irma Dumapit—thank you for trusting me

Elliot—your love, I have treasured. It's inside a small box of matches that I intend to up-cycle for my YouTube channel (may you rest in peace)

Jeremy Taylor you are my privilege

Jeremiah, my son - I love you

God—I bow in reverence to you

BEFORE I FORGET:
My cousins in the West Coast - Allan Ramis, Danny Ramis, Christine "Laka" Miranda, Edward Ramis. At a young age I've learned how to speak English—I thank God for your presence and influence in my life.

ABOUT THE AUTHOR

Marites Ong was born in the Philippines. The fifth child to her parents. When she was born—the doctor looked at her and the doctor fainted. Marites went down to the floor with the doctor, she rolled over the doctor's arms and hit her head on the cold cement de-livery room floor. She's not smart but determined. She managed to have graduated in col-lege with a degree in Bachelor of Science major in Computer Science at AMA Computer College in 1990.

Being a college graduate—she did not qualify to be employed at one of the many big com-panies in Singapore, they only accommodate university graduates. She thought—fuck it, I will go to America.

She took MAEd, she only finished one semester. This is due to lack of budget, more—she lacked the 3rd and 4th brain cells required to finish the course.

Her family don't belong to the elite of this world. Her parents were not a rich couple—only living paycheck to paycheck. She was just an ordinary person from an ordinary fami-ly—not like most special people are.

With her parents having six kids, she grew up witnessing the tight budgeting of her Mom. She went through hand-me-downs from her older sisters. It carved a sense of frugality in her as she grew. But in her heart, she kept the generosity from her Mom and the grit of her Dad.

Having considered her family belonging in the poor societal category from a third-world country. She dreamt that she would make it one day. She thought of going to America to work. She made it to America—but she did not make it big.

She considered herself as a person without any talent. But she's convinced that in America there's always another chance when the last one slipped away—another one is waiting just right around the corner.

She admired the works of John Grisham, Danielle Steel, Nora Roberts, Joan Rivers, Tom Clancy, Robert James Waller, C.S. Lewis and Jeremy Taylor. Although she doesn't have a good singing voice, she sings in the shower a lot.